Butch Cassidy came through the door holding the letter and a sheet of stiffer paper that was a wanted poster. He held out the letter. "Read it."

Lassiter was scratched from our wanted list last year. He was killed in a fire near the Mexican border. Body was identified by Sidney Blood.

Lassiter read it and laughed. The setup was ripe.

Our free catalogue is available upon request. Any Belmont/Tower titles not in your local bookstore can be purchased through the mail. Simply send 15¢ plus the retail price of the book and write Belmont/Tower Books, 185 Madison Avenue, New York, New York 10016.

Any titles currently in print are available in quantity for industrial and sales-promotion use at reduced rates. Address inquiries to our Promotion Dept.

LASSITER BANDIDO
JACK SLADE

Belmont/Tower Books • New York City

BANDIDO

A BELMONT/TOWER BOOK—October 1972

Published by

Belmont/Tower Books
185 Madison Avenue
New York, N.Y. 10016

Copyright © MCMLXVIII by Jack Slade

All rights reserved.

Printed in the United States of America

Chapter ONE

On May second Lassiter walked into the Antler saloon in Bridge, Montana. It was evening, warm. Noise in the rough room bounced off the bare wood walls. Outside, a distant train whistle from the east was lonely in the dark, empty street.

The saloon was nervous and jumpy, the noise was brittle, on the edge of panic. The town expected callers—had been expecting them for too long. They didn't know Lassiter; he could be one of the callers.

The woman in the red dress at the bar, without a glass, was standing alone. Even if he hadn't been hunting this woman Lassiter would have noticed her. There were about fifty men. Some were at the bar, at the poker tables and at the smaller tables. Some were drinking, some were laughing and some were watching the door. There were other women and none of them were alone. Only the woman in red stood by herself. The only empty spaces at the bar were on either side of her.

Lassiter went to the bar and took the place at her right. He ordered his drink. In the backbar mirror, he saw her big, gray eyes on him. He nodded at the bartender. "Give the lady a drink."

The man had a bottle in his hand as he turned away, and started down the bar. Lassiter, holding his glass, suddenly splashed the liquor against the back of the bartender's head. The man came around, caught the bottle by its neck, swung it loosely. Lassiter shoved his empty glass across the scuffed counter. "Fill it. Give the lady a drink."

The man was short and powerful through the shoulders. He wanted to slam the bottle across Lassiter's face. Then he met Lassiter's eyes and changed his mind. He filled the glasses and moved away.

The men at the bar saw and heard what was going on. They watched the bartender; they watched Lassiter. That section of the long room was suddenly quiet except for the tinny piano against the back wall.

The woman watch Lassiter. He looked her over—the short, low cut dress, the checkered stockings. Her voice, low, husky.

"You alone, mister?"

He smiled at her. "Alone."

"You're taking a long chance."

He put down his drink. The liquor wasn't good. In the mirror he saw that the men around him were tense, pretending no interest.

"Want to find a table, sit down?" he asked.

"You're a damned fool. Not in here."

"Where would you suggest?"

He read refusal in her face. Then her chin tilted up. Her eyes slid around the room. She lifted a full, bare shoulder. "Meet me down by the livery. Half an hour," she said.

She emptied her glass slowly, defiant, sashayed casually

toward the door and out into the night. Through the open door the train whistled. It was closer.

The livery corral was darker than the street, emptier than the street, and quiet. The runway doors were closed. There was no light in the office. The only movement was among the horses at the hitch rail in front of the saloon. The only lights were from the saloon, from the station, and from the signal lamps in the freight yard. The train snaked in, making the only noise.

Lassiter watched it from the doorway of the feed store beside the saloon, watched it take on water, watched the switchman's bobbing lantern, watched the cars grind out. In all of this time no one came from the saloon. No one apparently would follow him.

He stepped out across the wooden sidewalk. His boot heels made too much clatter against the old boards. He walked down into the deep dust of the roadway and turned toward the corner of the livery. He stopped there and looked behind him; still he saw no movement. Then he turned in at the side street beside the building.

The woman stood there, her back against the warped, unpainted planks. He saw only the white blur of her face and shoulders. Wind, hot, sudden, swept up the street, grabbed at her skirt. It flapped up, above legs that he could not see.

She said, "Stranger."

"Stranger." He touched her arm, firm, soft, warm. "Where can we talk?"

There was a tautness in her voice yet it was empty of hope. "Why talk?"

"Where?"

Without words she turned, moved down the ruts of the street into the rising, brush grown, open land.

The cabin was small, a single room built of logs, half the chinking fallen out. But it was clean and neat. He saw it from the doorway where he stopped until she lit the lamp. The lamp's beaded glass shade was an odd note of elegance in these parts.

He stepped over the sill and pushed the door shut. She did not speak but undressed immediately. When she turned toward him he noticed she was gold-toned in the lamplight, well-formed, broad and strong through the hips.

The bed was poor—a thin mattress stuffed with hay. He did not care. For weeks he had ridden the high, cold hills, alone. The woman, too, knew the commanding hunger of the body. They took their relief in surging demand. They drained themselves of need. But when they lay apart, naked, close in what should have been companionship, her spirit had not lifted. There was no hope in her voice, only a guarded curiosity. "Why did you pick me?"

He lied. "You were alone. A woman like you shouldn't be alone. Not in a saloon. Why did you call me a fool?"

"Because I'm poison. They're afraid to touch me while Johno is still alive. They're afraid even to serve me drinks." Bitterness shook in the words, burning, deep. "Even when he's in jail they're afraid. Even when he's going to be hanged they don't dare."

"If he's that bad off what are they afraid of?"

"He's one of Butch Cassidy's men. They don't know whether or not Butch will ride in and rescue him. They don't know who you are. Did you see the way they watched you?"

"I saw." He rolled out of the bed, dressed, rang a twenty dollar gold piece on the wash stand. "Get some clothes on to ride in. I'll be back for you."

She nodded slowly. She did not understand, but she was used to obeying orders. Any orders.

He went back into the night. He walked the half mile out of town, picked up the horses, rode in and tied them in the brush behind the cabin.

Thirty minutes later he slapped back the doors of the saloon and went in. The room was still filled with noise. But all of it, even the piano, stopped when he entered. He walked with exaggerated care, a drunken, barely balanced course toward the bar. Sawdust on the floor did not kill the sound of his steps. He faltered, grabbed the counter for support, and ordered the drink, his voice thick.

The bartender was sullen, slow in pouring. Lassiter drank quickly, turned over the glass and tried to shove it across the bar. "Nother," he said.

The man glared. "You've had enough. Go back to Hope. Sleep it off."

Hope . . . a funny name for a woman who knew no hope. Lassiter's hand was fast. He reached across, caught the dirty apron, yanked the fat stomach against the back edge of the counter. He hit hard. The bartender fell down.

Lassiter stumbled into the man beside him. The man threw a punch at Lassiter's head. Lassiter ducked. Then he hit the man in the stomach.

The room was sudden bedlam. The tension broke. They surged forward and crowded Lassiter to the corner. There were too many of them. Fists drove at him; he couldn't duck them all.

A big man with a star on his shirt stood up from a poker table, pushed ponderously through the mauling crowd. Lassiter was on the floor. He had been kicked three times in the ribs, once in the face.

The sheriff thrust the crowd back, stooped and hauled Lassiter to his feet. "You're drunk. Clear out of here," he said.

Lassiter wiped his mashed lips with the back of his left

hand; blood dripped onto the rough skin. Lassiter stared at the blood then buried his right fist in the sheriff's stomach.

The blow drove the sheriff back a step but did not knock him down. He drew his gun and brought the heavy barrel down along the side of Lassiter's skull. Lassiter collapsed, unconscious.

Chapter TWO

The cell was square, cramped with two tiers of bunks and a slop pail. It was lighted by a wall lamp in the empty outside office. It stank with the odors of drunks, unwashed men off the trails and with the acrid overlap of lysol.

The light hurt Lassiter's eyes. He rolled away from it, groaning, and lay muttering to himself.

"Shut up," he heard someone call.

Lassiter opened his eyes; it hurt to move the lids. He turned his head to a big man bracing an elbow on the bunk opposite. His hair was yellow, thickly curled; his eyes were round, blue.

Lassiter touched the ridge raised by the sheriff's gun. That hurt too. There was not much about him that did not hurt. He cursed in a running monotone.

"Shut up, I say. How can a man sleep?" the other yelled.

Lassiter shut up. He swung his feet to the floor and sat, looking around the cell, looking at the iron bars that walled it off from the office. There wasn't any privacy in this jail. He got to his feet, feeling his knees shake, feeling the wave of weakness. Avoiding touching the other man's bunk, he worked strength back into his muscles. He stopped before the bars, looked through to the office and the desk there. He saw his belt and gun lying on the desk, saw no one in the outer room. Still exercising his back and his legs, he turned, went to the bunk where the yellow-haired man lay watching. He gave the man a painful, twisted smile. "You like this lousy place?" he asked.

Johno Wade gaped at him, the surprise in his blue eyes genuine. "That's a pretty stupid question."

Lassiter lifted his shoulders. "Why stay?"

The eyes widened. "You must be a nut of some kind."

Lassiter's smile came again. "Want to leave with me?"

"Quit talking crazy. I'm slated to hang next week."

"Go pile up the mattresses in the corner by the door."

Wade did not move. Lassiter picked up the mattress from his bunk, slung it toward the far corner. "Put the others against it. Do it before somebody comes," he said to Wade.

Wade moved then. He didn't know what, but something about this madman was convincing. He stacked the straw ticks together, then went to the window where Lassiter was working.

Lassiter had his arm through the window bars, and was feeling below the sill. He found the end of the fuse that he had wedged into a crack between the stones of the wall, loosened it and pulled it inside. He struck a match and held its flame against the fuse. "Get back. Brace yourself," he said.

The fuse caught, sputtered. Johno Wade stared at it. said, "Where the hell did that come from?" Then without waiting for an answer ran to the mattresses and burrowed under them.

Lassiter hoped that no one would come into the office

just now. He let the burning fuse slide out of the window and drop, pulled himself up and pressed his cheek against the bars so he could look down. He held his breath. If the fuse went out when it hit the alley dust. . . .

It did not go out. The little sparks ate along it, following the twisting path toward the cache of dynamite he had buried at the base of the wall.

Lassiter watched until he was very sure that his plan would not be interrupted. Then he dived across the cell, under the mattress pile, holding the ticks down on top of them. He did not catch Johno's muttered question. It was lost in the sharp explosion that filled the alley.

The stone wall came apart, sagged, tumbled down. Part of the wooden roof caved in. Lassiter threw the ticks aside, jumped to his feet. Flames were already licking through the tangle of pitch filled rafters. He hauled Wade up, shoved him ahead toward the fire. Wade pulled back and Lassiter put a hand on his shoulders, and followed the stumbling figure through the flames.

He picked the man up from where he sprawled in the alley, and shook him to attention. "There are three horses in the bush behind Hope's cabin. I'll meet you there in five minutes. Get the girl in a saddle."

He shook the man once more, started him off with a shove, ran around the corner and in through the front door of the jail, caught up his gunbelt from the desk, and slapped it around his lean hips.

No one had appeared so far. He got a second belt and gun from a wall peg, jumped back to the street. Behind him fire was falling from the roof above the office. He stopped at the door for a fast look along the street.

The saloon crowd had not rushed out to investigate the explosion. They figured it was Cassidy's bunch, and none of them wanted to be in gun range. They stayed behind cover, waiting.

Lassiter ran. As he passed in front of the saloon, he bent over. Someone snapped a shot as he crossed the path of light, but the shot went high. Then he was in darkness, around the corner. He made a dash for the end of the side street.

Wade was already in the saddle, Hope on a horse beside him. Lassiter caught the third horse and flung up, driving it out before he was seated, turning to see the others wheel and fall in behind.

He kept the fast pace for a mile, for insurance, but there was no pursuit. No one in Bridge wanted to charge into these hills. Cassidy's fifty men might be out there, waiting to cut down anyone riding after Wade.

Lassiter dipped down a draw, slowed, followed it off the trail five miles from town. He was sure by then that it was safe to stop.

He swung down. He made no offer to help the girl, but left that to Wade. He did not want any trouble with Johno.

Lassiter made a small fire, got the coffee pot from his bedroll, filled it at the stream and put it to boil. The water was not good; it had a brackish odor and the smell of the cattle that waded in it further up its course. But boiled with enough coffee grounds it could be drunk.

Wade impatiently stood watching. He waited only until Lassiter sat back on his heels, and rolled a cigarette. Then Wade burst out. "All right. Just who the hell are you?"

Lassiter took his time. Looking up, his smile thin, he answered. "It matter to you?"

"Damn right. You were all set up to blow that wall before you got tossed in the cell. I want to know why."

"Wanted you out. Quickest way to get you."

Suspicion made Wade step back. "What for?"

"So you can take me to Butch Cassidy."

"Take you . . . ?" Wade's mouth dropped. Then he laughed, high, raucous. "You picked on the wrong boy, mister. I can't take anybody to Cassidy."

Lassiter put it down to the normal caution of an outlaw. He said softly, "Sure you can. You're his man."

He did not like the secret smile Wade gave him. There was some sour meaning behind it. The man did not answer. The woman watched Lassiter, and looked at Wade. She said in sudden disgust. "Because Johno was stupid. He got jealous of Herb Garnett and shot him in the Antler saloon."

Wade swung on her. "You stood there and gave him the glad eye. . . ."

She ignored him, talked on to Lassiter. "Stranger, Butch has a quiet deal with all the local law. The Wild Bunch don't make trouble in the towns, so they're allowed to ride in and out as they please. Johno broke the rule, shot a town man. Butch could have broken him out the next day, but he said the hell with him, let him hang."

Lassiter flipped his cigarette into the fire, kept the surprise out of his voice. "You didn't tell me that."

"You didn't ask."

The note in her voice brought up Wade's suspicion. "How come you two know each other?"

Her chin came up. "I met him in the saloon tonight."

The big man's hand went to the gun on his hip, the gun Lassiter had thrown to him when they rode out. Lassiter got himself set. The man was quartered to him, his attention on the girl. There was time to move. He stayed quiet, waiting. Wade's voice was a vicious rumble. "You let him pick you up?"

She lied easily, out of long practice. "I wanted to get you out. He said he could."

Wade's head swung slowly. Lassiter watched Wade's wild but puzzled eyes. He waited out the moment. Wade's hand eased, fell away from the gun. Lassiter stood up, but did not move his hands. Then he went to the saddle pack, found the tin cup, brought it back and filled it. Deliberately he offered it to Wade. The man took it, passed it to the girl. Lassiter filled it again for the big man, filled it a third time for himself. He drank, letting time run on. The hot liquid seared the cuts inside his bruised mouth. He sounded thoughtful, sympathetic. "You got trouble. I don't think Butch is going to like you running around loose. You'd better take me up there."

Wade yowled. "You're crazy. He'd kill me straight off."

Lassiter's head moved from side to side. "Not if you tell him how to pick up two tons of gold. Two tons. Half a million dollars. You'd be right popular."

"In a bank?" he asked.

"On a train."

"What train? When?"

Lassiter's lips thinned. "My ace. I know. Cassidy doesn't."

Johno Wade did not think fast. "If you know why do you want to tell Cassidy?"

"I need men. Could you carry two tons of gold out of these mountains alone? I can stop the train, but I need men to move the gold."

He glanced from Wade to the girl. Her breath had

drawn in sharply. Her eyes held more life than since he had met her.

"Sound nice? Would Cassidy like it?"

Wade spoke. "Like hell. It smells. It's sucker bait. You just want to get into the Hole."

"No." It was the girl's voice.

Wade watched, talked to the girl, his grin sour. "Yes. You got any idea how many railroad detectives have tried to weasel into the camp? A lot. Butch has killed plenty of them. I say this one is Wells Fargo."

Lassiter thought of Sidney Blood, special agent for the express company, dedicated to tracking him down. He thought of the years Blood had been on his trail. Blood wouldn't take it kindly that Lassiter was being taken for a company man. Lassiter laughed. "Think a minute, Johno. If you let this get away from Cassidy, I'll see that he hears about it. He won't like your making his decisions."

The girl caught Wade's arm. "Listen to me, Johno. He's no law man. I can smell that kind a country mile. Take him to the Hole. It's your only chance to get back with the Bunch, ever. If Butch decides he's a phony he can handle him himself."

The big man stayed suspicious, stubborn. "Nothing doing. I ride close to that canyon and a guard will shoot me down on sight."

Lassiter looked at the girl. "Would he shoot a woman?"

Wade's eyes lighted. "Maybe not. That might work."

"No." The girl gasped, frightened.

"Yes." Wade caught her arm, twisted it. "You're the one that's for this game. You'll ride in." He let go of her arm, cuffed her head with the palm of his hand as he would cuff a dog, knocked her over.

She took it in silence, looked up at Lassiter with appeal

in her eyes. Lassiter did not move as he watched her. His voice was flat. "Tell Cassidy the gold will be shipped on the Oriental Express in an ordinary baggage car. When I see him I'll tell him the date. He can't find out without me."

Chapter THREE

Everybody in three states talked about the Hole-In-The-Wall. Few had ever been there. It was as hard to get into as the Denver Mint.

A jewel of a valley, it had plenty of fresh running water, lush grass, and protection from the major blast of the wind off the northern high country. It was guarded by nature, walled away by jagged mountains, and the road in wound through a canyon through which only one rider could squeeze at a time. Beyond the upper end stretched fields of trailless badlands, miles of rock ridges, and pot holes. It was a land of lava pumice; it was leached, barren, and bleak.

Butch Cassidy held the valley for the nest of vipers the country called the Wild Bunch.

The government, egged by the railroads and express lines, had twice sent cavalry to clean it out. Cassidy's guards, hidden at the crest of the jumbled stone walls, had sent down their warning to Cassidy. The outlaws had gone into the badlands, scattered leaving no track on the hard surface of lava bed. It was impossible to follow them.

Confidently the soldiers had fired the log cabins, burned out the store, ridden away. Before they were clear of the canyon Cassidy's men were back, rebuilding their town on the smoking ashes.

The town was a going concern again when Lassiter was herded in. It looked like a comfortable, normal community. It didn't look like a death house.

They were tied together in a string. Lassiter's holster was empty, his hands lashed to his saddle horn. Ahead of him Johno Wade rode, bound on his mount, hunched in the saddle, waiting for a bullet. Behind, a three-man guard had no need of reins. There was no place for the horses to stray. The guard carried their rifles ready to use.

The canyon opened on the meadow. The grassy road became a grassy street. The horses followed it until the guard stopped them at the store.

Butch Cassidy's chair on the high gallery was tipped back against the log wall. He wore no hat. His eyes, hazel, leveled with Lassiter's. Lassiter knew him by reputation. Now he could judge for himself.

Throughout the west no outlaw was more talked about, yet he was a man of mystery. Express companies, stage lines, railroads, big ranch owners were robbed by him. Systematically he drained them, and amassed a legendary fortune. Yet the small merchants, the one horse ranches were safe. Cassidy did not permit his followers to harass the little towns, the little fellow. For two reasons: firstly, the profit was picayune; secondly, the small towns gave him a safety zone, room in which to move outside the valley.

This was his strength; this rule he imposed. This rule Johno Wade had broken in drunken forgetfulness.

The hazel eyes were cold glass marbles. They shifted

from Lassiter to Wade. Wade shriveled as if the eyes burned him.

Cassidy's voice was toneless. "Take him up the valley and shoot him."

Two of the guards closed on Wade. Wade did not beg. He knew Cassidy, knew begging was no use. He glanced accusingly at Lassiter.

Lassiter said quickly, "Wait a bit, Cassidy."

Cassidy took time in bringing his eyes around again, lowering them over the man on the horse, lifting them to his face. "Who the hell are you?"

"Lassiter."

"Never heard of you." But the eyes had flickered.

"You've heard of me. You've got a man planted in Wells Fargo's San Francisco office. He keeps you posted."

The bandit did not deny it. The tiny twitch of his lip suggested that he was pleased. "You know that much, you ought to know people don't just ride in here and make themselves at home. It's been tried. A lot of detectives have tried. Most of them are dead."

Lassiter made no comment. He had heard that Cassidy liked to talk. He wanted him to talk. Talk delayed, diluted sudden action, sudden death.

Silence ran long. Almost too long. The guard's rifle made a slow, silent arc, and anchored on Lassiter. The finger tightened on the trigger. Then Cassidy winked at the guard, and spoke to Lassiter. "What are you doing here?"

Lassiter relaxed. "Hope told you what. Two tons of gold."

"What made you spring Johno out of jail?"

"Hope told you that too. To bring me up here."

"He could have got you both shot instead."

"I didn't know that then. But it was a help. If I'd ridden in alone one of your smart boys would have knocked me out of the saddle."

"They still may. After I do a little checking in San Francisco."

"Check all you want, but make it fast."

At last, Cassidy chuckled. "I will. I will. Now about this gold, is it worth going after?"

Lassiter lifted one eyebrow. "Depends on what you think is worthwhile. Me, I kind of like the sound of half of a million. Nice warm figure."

Cassidy moved his shoulders against the wall. His expression did not change. From his manner Lassiter could not tell whether or not he was impressed. At least he was curious.

"Well, what's your story?"

Lassiter shifted his weight, but kept watching Cassidy. He took a breath. "I'm tired of this saddle. I don't like being tied. I came here to talk, but I do better out of the sun."

The hazel eyes did not blink. They had a quality that made them seem lidless, and his thoughts did not come out through them. It was still a long minute before he gave the order. One guard dismounted, and cut the thongs from Lassiter's wrists with a knife.

Lassiter did not massage the wrists though they burned as circulation forced through the veins. He did not dismount at once, but jerked his head toward Johno Wade. "Turn him loose," he demanded.

That brought a reaction. Cassidy sat forward. The chair legs came down hard. "What?"

"I told him he wouldn't be hurt when you heard about the gold."

Both corners of Cassidy's thin lips pulled down. "You giving orders here now?"

"Do you want two tons of gold?"

The hazel eyes burned. Lassiter met them, challenged the other's will. Cassidy shrugged. "All right. All right."

His finger flicked to the guard. Wade was cut free. The big man fumbled out of the saddle, stood clinging to the horse, his knees too shaky to hold him up. He looked at Lassiter not quite believing himself still alive. Then in a surge he shoved back, ran up the grass street toward the cabins above. Cassidy's laugh cawed after him. Cassidy came out of his chair, came down the steps, arrogantly beckoned, and then, walked toward a cabin.

This, the largest in the town, had three rooms—a kitchen, a bedroom, and a living room which had a stone fireplace. Indian blankets in bright geometric patterns draped the walls, covered the chinked logs. The chairs were handmade. They were crafted by the men who in their fight against boredom were often compelled to wait here until the outside law cooled down and went home.

Lassiter looked at the polished leather seats with backs of woven cowhide strips. He looked at the furnishings—all sturdy, functional, unembellished. Yet there was a grace to the room. He thought again about the man who lived here.

Some claimed that Cassidy was the son of a Mormon rancher. Others insisted he was the black sheep scion of an old and respected Boston house. Whatever, he was no ordinary road agent. His work showed imagination, flare, daring, and scope. Scope was what Lassiter counted on. That Cassidy would comprehend an operation of this size, would go into it with hardheaded vision, and not blunder in like a dazzled fool.

He was relying for his judgment on the strength of two stories about the man. One, that he had rustled six hundred horses from a Montana ranch, shipped them east in the cars of a bankrupt circus and sold them to the Boston Street Railway Company at the legal going rate per head. In another robbery he was said to have held up the Silk Express out of Seattle, shuttled the rich bolts by pack horse down the Outlaw Trail to Mexico, and sailed it to Europe's hungry market.

Apparently he thrived on challenge. And so far as Lassiter knew Cassidy had never reached for half a million in gold at a single grab.

Cassidy set a bottle of whiskey, two glasses, on the hand hewn table, poured them full, dropped to a chair, and waved Lassiter to another. "Now. Let's hear what this is about."

Lassiter drank. The whiskey was good. He nodded appreciation. Then he spoke. "The shipment will come within the month. Six weeks at the outside. Accumulation from the Homestead mine. They haven't sent an ounce of gold out for months. There's been a fight to control the company. All production is being held at the mine."

Cassidy listened as if for a voice beyond Lassiter's, for ideas that were not in the spoken words. Much as he liked to talk, he could listen when he wanted to hear. He sounded more than skeptical. "I hadn't heard of it," he answered.

"Meaning your spy in San Francisco hasn't heard? He won't."

"Why?"

Lassiter let his pleasure glint in his eyes. "Because it's Sidney Blood's job to get it through. He's been made responsible. He made his own condition that no one in the home office would know about it until the shipment gets to Chicago."

Cassidy's eyes drooped. "How come you know?"

"I know."

"We can make you talk. We've got boys who learned how from the Apaches."

Lassiter took up the bottle, poured his glass full again, stopped when the liquid trembled above the edge of the rim. Another drop would have sent a small sluicing down the outside. He did not answer.

Cassidy tried another tack. "When is the shipment?"

"They haven't picked a date. I'll know when they do."

Cassidy's jaw muscles set. He did not like opposition. "You know so much, what do you want with me?"

It was a slip, a weakness. Cassidy knew well enough that a single man could not handle two tons of gold, get it down to Mexico alone. Lassiter played it straight. He did not want the outlaw resenting the fact that he had exposed himself.

"I'm a loner. I need men, animals, to get the stuff off the train and down the trail to a market. There's no single market for that much closer than the border."

"Good enough thinking. What about the split?"

Lassiter lifted the glass, and drank the amber liquid. "One quarter to me, three quarters to you. You take care of your crowd."

Cassidy did not bargain. Lassiter did not expect him to. The outlaw was not considering whether Lassiter would live to spend a share of the gold. His thoughts, not even pausing over the point, were already at the next step. "Where do we stop the train?"

"I've picked a place."

Cassidy heaved himself from his chair. The hazel eyes

glittered. "For a man sitting like a rat in a trap you don't shake out much information. I don't go at things this blind."

For the first time Lassiter smiled. "Don't expect you to. When you hear from San Francisco, when your agent tells you I'm not a Wells Fargo man out to ambush you, then we'll talk. How about giving me back my gun?"

"Not until I'm sure who you are."

"When will that be?"

"I've sent a man to town to wire. Answer ought to come in a couple of days," he said.

Chapter FOUR

Johno Wade felt like a man reborn. For days death had breathed down his neck—death from the law, death from Cassidy. Now the certainty of it was gone. He was not only free, but he was important again. He was the man who had brought in two tons of gold.

That it was not in their hands did not matter. The men of the Wild Bunch had complete faith in Butch Cassidy. They jammed against the rough store counter which doubled as a bar listening to Wade. Their laughter was heavy and loud. Johno's voice was louder. He wasn't yet tired of telling how Lassiter had blown out the jail wall. The men weren't tired of hearing it. There had been little excitement of late.

Around the walls of the big room the women waited. There were a lot of women in the valley. By Cassidy's ruling a man could bring in a woman, keep her as long as he wanted, get rid of her and bring in another. He could not have more than one at a time. Two women with one man asked for trouble, and Butch Cassidy did not like unnecessary trouble.

When Lassiter came through the open door he saw Hope standing apart from the others. They were alike in that they always stood apart from the crowd. She was by far the best-looking of the bunch. And the only one who stirred him. He glanced at the crowd, then walked to her under the watching eyes of her sisters.

She was startled, frozen in fright. She looked quickly to the bar. Johno Wade's raucous voice was boastful, strident, thick. Lassiter saw him leaning heavily on the bar; he knew that he would not be on his feet much longer.

He took Hope's arm, turned her toward the door. She held back, but then, not wanting a scene to attract Wade's attention, she went.

Outside, the moon rode high, lighted the valley, picked out the scant trees, and softened the ragged slopes. It did not ease Hope's fright. Fifty yards from the store she stopped. Her fear was in her voice. "Johno will kill you for sure."

"Johno is past the point of knowing." He put a finger beneath her chin, tipped her head up.

She shook free. "They'll tell him. The other women. They hate me."

He took her shoulder, pulled her to him. "Why?"

She had no more modesty than a child. She was artless. "Because I'm younger, prettier."

His fingers touched the soft, bare shoulders. "You are that. You're beautiful." She was not, but it didn't hurt to tell her so. Pride was all she had.

He felt her respond to his fingers, then she tried to pull back. But the hunger in her voice betrayed her words. "Listen to me. I tell you he'll kill you."

He covered her mouth with his lips, spoke against her ear. "You wouldn't care."

She thought about that. Then she said, "Yes. I would."
"Why?"
"I don't know . . . you're different . . . you don't hit me . . . hurt me."
"Maybe that's my weakness."

It sounded teasing. But it was almost an oath. Women were his weakness—all women. He could not resist them. And want was highest in him when there was jeopardy. He knew it, had tried to fight it, but had never won. Several women had nearly gotten him killed. This one might.

He turned her, led her up the grassy track between the rows of cabins. He found a clearing in the matted grasses. They would be sheltered behind rocks. He shed his clothes, watched her quickly pull off her blouse and skirt, watched the moonglow on her ripe body.

Her arms were warm against his naked back. Her thighs were strong. Although she had no intellect she had a rich perception of the demand sex put upon such men as he.

When they were spent, when they lay side by side, cooled by the soft night air, she whispered against his face. The whisper was muted by fear, terror that they might be found here.

"We can't do this again. If you don't care, I do. Johno promised that if he ever caught me he'd cut his brand on me."

He rolled to her again, more leisurely, and told her, "He's not man enough for you."

"No . . . not like you. . . ."

"We'll get you away from him."

"You're trying to get yourself murdered."

"He won't do anything here. He's afraid of Cassidy. Maybe not of anyone else, but Cassidy yes. And Cassidy will keep me alive until he gets that gold."

"After that?"

"He'll want me dead then. He'll want my share."

Part of her reaction was her body's surge. It was more violent with the impulse to escape. Then she sank back, whimpering, a child lost in the dark. The sound had no hope, no courage.

"He'll kill me too. I don't want to die . . . I don't. . . ."

"No." His voice cut through, harsh, reached her. "Do what I tell you and you won't be hurt. You'll be rich. Free."

She looked at him, blank, without comprehension. He repeated.

"Rich, Hope. Rich and free."

He tried to hold her longer. She would not stay. She got up, dressed as if in a dream, hardly seemed to hear him, did not believe. She had learned in childhood not to believe.

He watched her go, slip through the shadows, and disappear toward her cabin. The cool wind from the far peaks chilled him. He dressed. Then he lay back, folded his hands beneath his head, looked up, into the night sky, looked through it. The valley lay in peace. Deceptive peace. Unseen on the guardian peaks the sentinels watched. The only sound was drunken laughter from the store.

The first step was completed. He was inside the valley and still alive. Here he would sit on a powder keg until the thing was over. The opportunity had been long in coming. The plan was delicate. Simple, but delicate. To Lassiter it was worth the risks.

The delicate part was in finding the right messenger. He could not approach Blood himself. None of Cassidy's men would do. So he had chosen a woman. He could not tell her what her part was to be. He had waited too long for this chance to risk a slip. With Cassidy, there must be no possibility of his becoming suspicious.

Hope seemed a good choice. She was an outlaw's girl. She lived in the Hole-in-the-Wall. When she went to Blood with the story he would believe her.

The task, to bind Hope to him, would take doing. She was sufficiently greedy, but scared out of her wits. Still, there was no one else.

So he had started it. The stakes were high—the stake he offered was his life, he could die.

He stretched, stood up, and walked to the cabin.

The cabin assigned to him was at the head of the street. He did not share his cabin as did the others. Cassidy, not wanting to take chances, kept him apart. He did not trust his men when two tons of gold were involved—not until he was certain of Lassiter.

Lassiter passed Cassidy's dark cabin. The man might or might not be there. He had not appeared in the store. He could have been visiting a woman, could have ridden down canyon, could now be setting a trap, or could be selling Lassiter to a sheriff.

Lassiter did not light his lamp, and did not get into the bunk. Instead he threw his saddle on the thin reed mattress, covered it with the blanket, took a second blanket behind the stove, and stretched on the floor. This is where he slept.

Always he slept with an animal ability to wake at once, at any sound. The creak of door hinges brought his eyes open. Light came through the single window.

Johno Wade came in. He was hatless, his yellow hair a tangle. The smell of stale whiskey came with him. He balanced just inside the door, holding to it, swaying. His eyes fastened on the lump in the bunk, locked there. A club hung in one hand. Cassidy had not given him a gun.

He lurched forward, trying to be light on his feet. His

weight made the plank floor creak. Above the bunk he pitched forward, almost fell, straightened back, raising the club with both hands. He struck down. The blow would have broken a man's back.

He did not see Lassiter coil to his feet, catfoot to the door. The club was over his head for a second strike when Lassiter said,

"This way, Johno."

Lassiter did not want to be trapped in the small room with the huge man. He jumped through the doorway. Wade came around, nearly fell. A buffalo bellow filled the room. He charged. He thought Lassiter had run.

Lassiter had not. He stood at the right of the door, against the rough bark of the logs. His fist buried two inches into the bloated stomach as Wade came out.

Air exploded. Vomit came with it. Wade bent, paralyzed. For a moment only. He came around, the club swinging. Lassiter ducked. The club whistled over his head, crashed on the thick wall. The impact jarred it from Wade's hand. It spun off, landed fifteen feet away.

Lassiter hit again, again at the stomach. The paunch was the weakest spot. It had absorbed a lot of whiskey. Air and matter rushed out again. Wade grabbed at Lassiter, missed. Like a gorilla Wade crouched against the wall, long arms dangling, ending in huge hanging hands. He swayed. Suddenly lurched forward. The big hands swept out, reaching toward Lassiter's shoulders. Wade roared, wanting to drag Lassiter into his hug.

Lassiter jumped back, out of the reach. The man's rush carried him past. Lassiter kicked the knee cap. The leg gave. Wade went to his knees. Lassiter could have kicked at the head. Finished it then. He did not. Men were shouting, running toward the cabin. Cassidy was there. He would, Lassiter thought, stop the fight.

Cassidy made no move to interfere, only looked about him at the growing circle of men. They were laughing, yelling encouragement to Wade. They had not had this much excitement in weeks. It flashed to Lassiter that he had misjudged Cassidy. The outlaw would not let Wade kill him, not until the gold was safely in his hands, but he would not object to Lassiter being beaten close to death. It was too late for the kick to the head. Wade was up, circling, slow with new found caution. The liquor was driven out of him. He was an accomplished roughhouse fighter. Instinct, not brain, directed him. And his power was like a grizzly's.

Lassiter watched warily. His strength could not match the other's. He saw Wade come in, head low, meaning to butt. He let him come, waited for the moment, brought his boot up with vicious force. The toe caught Wade under the chin. It should have broken the neck. It did not.

Wade was jerked upright, then he came again. The long arms stretched before him, reaching. Lassiter dodged aside. Behind him a hand went between his shoulder blades. Pushed hard. It shoved him off balance, shoved him forward. He stumbled, kept from falling but could not escape.

Wade's arms closed about him, grappled him in the crushing embrace.

He brought up his shoulder. Hard. Under the chin again. Again Wade was jarred.

But the hold closed tighter. Wade's sour breath was in his face. Lassiter used a savage knee to the groin. Wade screamed. Pain twisted the heavy features. He did not relax. Lassiter expected his ribs to crack. He forked the fingers of his right hand, stabbed at the eyes.

Wade screamed again. This time the grip loosened. This

time he tried to step away, escape the rigid fingers in his eyes. Lassiter went with him. Shoved harder.

Wade clutched with both hands at Lassiter's wrist. Tried to pull the fingers away.

Lassiter took a fast step back, drove his right into the stomach, hit the man with his left under the ear.

Wade was all but blind. He fumbled forward. Lassiter hit him again, again. His whole weight in the blows. It was like pounding a rock. Chopping at a tree.

No one blow put the big man down. It was strike after strike. Hammering, hammering at the nearly senseless body. Finally Wade crumpled.

Lassiter stood over him. He could barely stand. He heard the crowd noise. It came from far off, from another world.

No one came to help him. No one helped Wade. They were turning away. The show was over. Their interest was gone.

A barrel stood beside the cabin, set to catch rain water from the roof. Lassiter walked to it. His legs felt disjointed. His hands burned, swollen. His chest burned.

He buried his head in the water. Held his breath as long as he could. He soaked his hands and arms. He filled the bucket that hung on the barrel. Poured it over himself, scrubbed at the blood, the mess from Wade. He used three buckets. He filled it a fourth time, carried it back, dumped it over Johno Wade.

The big man did not stir. His eyes were open, bloodshot, but he lay still.

The crowd was gone. There was no one in sight. Except Hope. She stood at the door of a cabin down the street. Lassiter stumped toward her, stiff-kneed to stay on his feet. Other women came to their doors as he passed, looked out at him. He took no notice.

Hope turned away, started into the cabin, started to close the door. Lassiter yelled. She stopped. He came against the log wall, propped himself against it. He needed it. He needed support.

The girl shrank back. "You keep away from me. . . ."

He stepped toward her. "Why? I licked him."

For answer she tore off her waist, turned, showed her back. Across the shoulders, burned with the redhot point of a knife was a blistered signature. Lassiter read *Johno*.

Chapter FIVE

Butch Cassidy yelled, "Haloo the house."

Lassiter, inside the cabin, thought the touch of civility suggested a good humor. Cassidy could have simply walked in. He would have had no need to fear startling the man inside. Lassiter still did not have his guns.

He had been at the Hole in the Wall for a week. He had not seen Cassidy since the fight with Johno Wade. He had not spoken to anyone except the storekeeper who sold him supplies. He had kept near his cabin, waiting for Wade to make another attack. The big man had not showed.

Cassidy came through the door holding the letter and a sheet of stiffer paper. His eyes on Lassiter were bright with mocking laughter.

"Our answer just came in. Read it."

Lassiter took the letter, read: *Lassiter was scratched from our wanted list last year. He was killed in a fire near the Mexican border. Body was identified by Sidney Blood. Check the picture on the enclosed dodger against your man.*

Cassidy handed over the dodger. The likeness was better than fair. "You could be his twin brother."

"I never had a twin." Lassiter kept the ice from his tone. "You satisfied that's my picture?"

Cassidy's smile twisted. "Maybe I could make a buck, turning you in."

Lassiter was casual. "Do that. And every man here will start looking at you sideways wondering if his turn will come up next. I thought you were smarter."

Cassidy laughed. Without amusement. "You're a cool one, friend. You like making enemies? You've already got one here. Wade would cut your throat the minute I let him."

"If he could. He'd need help."

"He might find that. He's got friends in the valley."

"And where's the profit to you?"

Abruptly Cassidy's manner changed. The hazel eyes were admiring, almost friendly. He flicked the letter with a fingernail.

"I guess you'll do. Now, what's the score?"

"My guns?"

Cassidy turned to the door, swung a beckoning hand. They went down the street, turned off at Cassidy's cabin. Cassidy crossed the room, took Lassiter's belt from a nail in the wall, watched Lassiter fasten it around his flat hips.

"Good looking rig. I had an idea of keeping it. Who made it for you?"

"Friend of mine in Weaverville."

But Cassidy seemed not to hear. His mind was already on something else. He said thoughtfully,

"I think we'd better get rid of Wade."

"Valuable to you, isn't he?"

"Not so much since that killing in Bridge. And both of you here means trouble. Why can't you let that girl of his alone?"

"Why should I?"

37

Cassidy snorted. "Women. They've got more men killed than Indians ever did. I'll run him out, see he's taken care of."

"Run him out. Don't kill him."

Cassidy's head came up, his eyes wide, suspicious. "What the hell? You that soft?"

"You think so?"

"I'm starting to wonder. You damn fool, Wade knows we're going after that gold shipment. In his shoes, what would you do if you were let out of here alive?"

"Hotfoot it to Sidney Blood, tell him we know about the transfer and are going to hit it."

Cassidy started a curse, changed his mind, stood waiting.

Lassiter added, "Let Wade know we plan to stop the train in Painter Canyon."

"Do we?"

"No. But it will make Blood happy. I like to keep Sidney happy."

"What's that supposed to mean? You know Blood?"

"Very well. He's been doing his best to get me trapped and hung for six years."

"And you want him to know you're in on this job?"

"I want him to know."

"Why?" It was an explosion.

"If he spends half his time worrying over how to catch me, and you, he'll have less to put in on protecting his train."

Cassidy was red with rising anger. "Can't you give a straight answer to anything?"

"When I know one, yes."

"Meaning what?"

"Meaning that Sidney Blood is not a fool. The minute

Wade tells him about our plan he's going to know someone talked. Nobody at his home office knows about the shipment except Lloyd Tevis, the president of Wells Fargo, and the head of their police force, James Hume. They're not apt to talk. So it had to come from either Spokane or the mine."

"Where did it come from?"

Lassiter looked at him.

Cassidy made an impatient gesture. "I don't care, damn it. Keep your secret if it makes you feel big. But what does it get us?"

"The gold." Lassiter smiled. "Just be sure Wade hears we're headed for Painter Canyon."

He went out, walked up past Wade's cabin. The door was shut, the curtains tight across the window. From behind his own window he watched the lower street. He was rewarded. Cassidy went to the store. Shortly, four men came from it, walked to Wade's, went in without knocking. Within minutes they appeared again, surrounding Wade. Wade was still in bad shape. His hands were tied at his back, he stumbled as he walked, was shoved back on balance and herded down to Cassidy's cabin just as Cassidy returned to it.

Lassiter waited until the door had closed behind them. Then he went to Wade's place. The girl Hope was rigid, sitting on the edge of the bunk, naked. Her fine figure was still as stone. She seemed to listen, for shouting, for horses drumming out of the valley, for a shot. Her eyes widened in blank fear when Lassiter filled the door, came in.

Sight of her body pulled at his urgency. He crossed to her, kissed her cheek, but the time for passion was not yet. He was here on business. His voice was hard, to bring her attention alive.

"They've taken Johno to Cassidy."

"I know." The words were a whisper. The lips did not move. "They're going to kill him."

"Not this time."

Her eyes came up, shocked. "No?"

"No. I told them not to."

Terror filled her face then, filled her voice. "For God's sake. Why? Why?"

He stepped back, pretending surprise. "For you. I thought you loved him."

An animal cry broke from her, throaty, despairing. "Love? Love? A woman like me can't afford love."

"Then why did you stay with him?"

She looked at him then as if she saw him for the first time, as if the fact of him had just registered on her. She frowned, not believing that he did not know the answer, told him as she would tell a child.

"A woman like me has to have a man. One man. I don't have a chance in this world without a man."

His slow smile started, spread. He lowered himself, hunching down before her, careful not to break the chain of her thought by any quick movement. He put out a lean forefinger, laid it on her knee, pressed it there.

"Yes. You do. With enough money you don't need any man. Hope, I can get you that money."

For a brief moment her eyes lighted, then the light faded. She had heard promises like this before. Before the light was gone he was talking again.

"Help me. I need your help. I'll pay for it, enough to keep you free for the rest of your life."

The light came back, trembled there, dimmed. Her voice was thin with uncertainty.

"Why should I trust you? What do you want?"

He rose smoothly, evenly, pressed her back on the bunk,

kissed her as he dropped his trousers, took her, talked to her, trying to break through.

"I'll make you rich, Hope. My promise. I keep my word."

"I still don't know what you want me to do."

"I'll tell you when the time comes. It will be easy. Safe for you."

After a long while she sighed, surrendered, and said against his ear. "All right, Lassiter. All right."

Chapter SIX

In Butch Cassidy's cabin the outlaw was putting on a show. He had, he thought, quite a talent for acting, and the flair came in handy. Partly it served to amuse him. Among all those who followed him there was not one with the brain, the imagination, to be considered an equal. No one to comprehend the deliberate irony in his feats. No one to appreciate the mastery with which he flourished his disdain of the human race. The men never caught on how viciously he was mocking them, that they were to him no better than trained animals being put through intentionally degrading circus acts.

His showmanship was useful too. It kept the restless, lawless crowd in tight control. By practice he had perfected the art of the tirade.

He was using it now on Johno Wade, with Johno's escort for audience. Later they would repeat it in the store with a touch of awe. A good way to spread the gospel.

Johno sat on a chair in the middle of the room. He sweat. Terror oozed from him. It made a stench in the room. He wore no shirt. His face, his body, were swollen, marked, discolored in red, black, blue splotches that advertised Lassiter's beating. One eye was closed. A gash along one cheek, healing slowly, still wept.

Cassidy's words had lashed him for an hour. Cassidy kept walking around him, his lips curved in an exaggerated sneer. The gold flecks in the hazel eyes danced with derision.

"God, you're an ugly sight. Have you looked at yourself? I can't stand to look at you. I can't think of one reason why you ought to be left alive. Can you?"

Wade's thick tongue ran around his bruised lips like a red mouse hunting a place to hide. He tried to answer. He could only croak. He fully expected to die. Yet now Cassidy seemed to be holding out a thread of hope. If he could answer. If he could. . . .

Cassidy snorted, stopped in front of him. "I'd like to think of some nice fresh way to get shut of you. Something that would be remembered. But you happen to be in luck. First things come first with me. My mind's busy." He tapped his temple with a curved forefinger. "I've got two tons of gold coming down Painter Canyon to think about. So. . . ." He snapped his fingers behind him, at the guards. "Bring up a horse. Load this lump of nothing aboard. Shove him out of the canyon." He brought his hands forward, wagged the finger between Johno's eyes. "And you . . . if I ever catch a look at you again, you've had it."

Luck. Johno had caught at the word. Twice now luck had snatched him back from the grave. Luck when Lassiter had busted him out of the Bridge jail, luck now. Luck came in threes. He decided to press for the third stroke. His burning rage at Lassiter was not only for the beating. There was also the man's making free with Hope. He might, he thought, even a part of the score now. He risked looking up at Cassidy.

"Anything you say, Butch. Can I take my girl?"

Cassidy started to shake his head. He stopped. Lassiter wanted that woman. Getting rid of her would be a way of showing him who was boss here.

"Welcome to her. Get her out of here and tell her not to come back."

Wade backed out of the cabin, bobbing his gratitude. He ran up the grassy street, brushed open his door, shouted his news.

He paid no attention to the fear she showed, the arguments she cried at him. He threw her few things at her, cursed at the way she dawdled in wrapping them in the blanket, pushed her out to the horses the guards were holding outside.

She sat on the horse, looking back at Lassiter's cabin, willing him to see what was happening. Then Johno cut her animal's flanks with a strap, it leaped, ran with the others toward the canyon mouth. The last glimpse she had was of the street, empty. Lassiter had not even stepped outside his door.

At the bottom of the canyon the guards stopped, wheeled, waited there, watched. Johno Wade drove the girl ahead of him, rode out across the rolling hills toward the west. Hope looked numbly at the future, made more empty, ugly now for having dared believe that Lassiter would help her.

Behind, in the valley, Butch Cassidy stood on the porch, watched the group ride out until the canyon swallowed it. Then, smiling, he walked to Lassiter's cabin. The devil in him wanted to gloat now over this man whom he had not been able to frighten.

Lassiter was at the pot bellied stove making coffee, frying meat. He heard the latch lift, swung, the smoking skillet in one hand, half expecting Hope to come in. His expression did not change as he saw Cassidy. He emptied the meat onto a tin plate, found a cold biscuit in the box, poured two cups of coffee, shoved one across the table. It was his only greeting. He sat down and began to eat.

Cassidy closed the door, crossed, reached for the second cup. He said idly.

"Wade's gone. Likely he's making a bee line to your friend Sidney Blood. Just the way you wanted it." He paused, then added, "He took his woman with him. She didn't want to go."

His eyes were careful on Lassiter's face, watching for reaction. There was none. Not even a break in the rhythmic chewing. Lassiter finished the meat, softened the biscuit in his coffee, ate that slowly with the deliberate attention of a man starving, bent on enjoying the last crumb. He finished the last of his coffee, wiped at his lip, stood up.

"She isn't his any longer. She's mine."

He turned to the bunk, began rolling his gear in the blanket. Cassidy watched. His eyes brightened with pleasure.

"Where do you think you're going?"

"After the woman."

Cassidy laughed. He had put down his cup. His hand rested lightly on the butt of his gun.

"Like hell you are. You're not leaving this valley until it's time to find out how that gold is coming through. And then I'm going with you."

Lassiter straightened. His brows raised. He looked more questioning than disturbed.

Cassidy nodded toward the wall. "I'll take those guns again, just to keep you honest."

The gunbelt was hanging from a nail. Lassiter went to it, lifted the heavy weapons, balanced them as if not quite certain what he wanted to do. Cassidy did not move other than to slide his fingers around to grip his own gun. It seemed a battle of wills. Lassiter sighed. Apparently Cassidy had won. Lassiter extended his guns butt first.

Cassidy took them one at a time, thrust them into his waistband. The hazel eyes glinted with satisfaction.

"Maybe you're beginning to get the idea of who runs this place. I'll let you pick up a woman first time we go outside." He walked to the door, went out whistling.

Lassiter turned back to the bunk, finished his bundle. His lips were curved, almost smiling.

An hour later he went to the store for tobacco. He lingered on the porch, aware that he was watched from all angles of the street, hen stepped down into the track. In full sight of the town he walked toward the mouth of the canyon.

Where the walls narrowed in a man sat on a rock up the hillside. Sun caught the rifle across his knees. Cassidy was blocking that exit of the valley. Lassiter smoked a cigarette, returned back up the street. He passed the big pole corral where all of the horses were kept. A guard was there too. He grinned as Lassiter passed. There was hunger in the grin.

Lassiter winked at him, passed on, went leisurely to his cabin. At dark he cooked his supper, ate, went out. The riders were gathering at the store for their nightly drink. He followed them, filled a cup at the keg, carried it to a corner, lowered himself to a pile of sacks.

From along the wall the women watched him, some curious, some mocking, all showing their smugness that

Hope was gone. The men watched him too, equally openly. The word had spread that Cassidy had put this interloper in his place. They were wolves, ready to tear down anyone who did not belong to their pack. Lassiter did not belong. He had no friend in this room, in this valley. He didn't want one.

No one had spoken to him by midnight. He rose and went to his cabin, left the light unlit, lay down on the bunk fully dressed and pulled a blanket over him. Moonglow made a square on the wall where the window was. Lassiter watched that. Within minutes the shape of the square changed. A man's head blanked out part of the light. A face came against the glass, stayed there motionless, silent.

Lassiter rolled over, flung the blanket, made certain that the watcher knew he was there. Satisfied, the man went away. Lassiter lay for another hour. No one else came. He rose and went outside. He stood revealed in the white light, studied each of the pockets of shadow, covered his interest by the performance of an innocent function. He was not, apparently, under further watch.

The moon subsided behind the canyon rim. Darkness congealed in the valley. Lassiter moved through it. His boots were silent on the thick grass. None of the cabins showed light now. The camp slept. Except for the guards. On the crests, at the narrows of the trail, at the corral, men would be awake, alert.

Lassiter carried a coil of rawhide rope. He went toward the corral. Inside the bars the animals moved fitfully. They covered any sound the man might make. He smelled their nearness, put out a hand, found himself against the fence, stood listening.

The wait was long. He began to believe that the guard had been withdrawn, began to move. Then a light flared.

Very small. At the far side of the enclosed acre. A match struck to light a cigarette.

Lassiter turned along the fence. The horses sensed him, shied away. He retreated, made a wider swing, judged his distance from the guard, stopped to wait for the man to betray his position again. A second match flared ten feet ahead. Lassiter covered the space in a soundless run.

His arm went around the throat, dragged the head back, choked off a yell. The side of his other hand chopped at the stretched neck. The man went limp. Lassiter dropped him. He took the short gun from the guard's holster, left the rifle. He needed his hands free.

He found the corral gate, opened it and went through, dallied his rope, built a loop. The horses crowded away, circled as he advanced. With so little light he could not choose the one he wanted. He took the first over which he could throw his loop.

The horse was trained. It stopped as soon as it felt the rawhide. He worked to it, hand over hand, closed his fingers over the flared nostrils, quieted the animal, fashioned a hackamore with the lariat, led the horse from the corral. He left the gate open. The other mounts would soon slip through it with the instinct to escape, would spread through the valley. It would take the riders some time to recapture them.

He headed for his cabin, the saddle and bridle there. It was still far up the street when a man loomed out of the dark before him, his surprised cry broke the silence. Lassiter had not expected a relief guard at this hour. But the damage was done. The warning was sounded.

He shot the guard, saw him drop, struggle on the ground. He left him, flung himself on the horse's back, kicked it up the street.

Sound roiled ahead of him. Cries. Doors slapping open. Shots. The outlaws slept lightly. Any shot meant trouble.

Lassiter raked the horse, felt it leap forward under him. He laid low on its neck, ran the gamut between the cabins. He passed his own door. No time now to stop for gear. The valley behind him was alive with running, shouting men. He raced on, toward the badlands, the only avenue open to him. Without saddle, bridle, water, food, hat.

The ground turned rough. The grass thinned, stopped. The horse's hoofs struck sparks from the bare rock. Lassiter could see little. He must trust the animal to find safe footing.

Within ten miles dawn came, showed him a tumbled sea of sharp broken lava ridges, coarse beds of pumice and volcanic ash. There was no vegetation here, no indication of water. No sign of any life.

He pushed on. The sun came, a glowing red ball. It laid red paths on the black rock. The glass smooth surfaces reflected sheets of brilliance, blinded him.

He used the sun as guide, urged the horse. He wanted as many miles as possible between him and the valley before the rising heat would send up waves, distort distance, confuse direction.

He crossed a high ridge, looked back from its vantage point. In the far distance riders moved, crisscrossing each other, searching the brakes. Pursuit did not worry him. Gathering their horses had cost them much time, and his horse left no trail on this unyielding rock. They would turn back when they did not find him before noon. They had hidden in this brutal land themselves. They knew his chance for survival here without water. It was not high.

Noon came and passed. Lassiter pulled off his shirt, draped it over his head. It did little to deflect the strength of the sun's heat. Heat became an element of itself, a visible, boiling ocean, shimmering, waving around him.

His tongue swelled. His eyes puffed. The horse wilted as moisture evaporated from it. Ahead there was no end to the heaving, rigid waves of black glass. There was no growth. Not even a barrel cactus. Even had there been, he had no knife with which to cut out the top, scoop out the damp pulp to wet his parched throat.

The sun moved down slowly. An hour before it would sink he found a patch of shade in the lee of a knife-sharp ridge. The air burned his lungs still, but he escaped the direct stab of the rays. He curled on the ground, away from the rock face that blistered the hand.

From extreme heat the land turned cold with darkness. The wind chilled him, but it was dry, searing.

He rested the horse, slept, went on to use the night hours, and hoped to find shelter to wait out the next day. He found none. The serried ridges broke ahead as far as his vision went. The mounds of ash piled higher. The horse floundered through the sharp powder. It was worse going than the hard rock. He dismounted, led the animal. The sun crept overhead.

The lariat jerked, went taut, held. Lassiter stopped, looked back. His eyes were swollen shut. He forced the lids open. The horse was down, had stepped into a pothole, broken its leg. It lay still, made no attempt to rise.

Lassiter used the short gun. He located the jugular vein, and put a single shot through it. Then he knelt, put his mouth against the gushing flow of hot blood, and swallowed with spare, careful sips.

He bathed his face, his arms, his body. He dared not bathe his feet. Once he took them off, he would not again be able to pull on the boots.

He drank again. He searched the ground, found a head-sized chunk of lava, hurled it against the pothole edge. On the third cast it shattered. A sharp-edged silver broke from it. He used it as a knife, cut into the dead horse, gouged meat from it. There was nothing with which to make a fire. He ate the meat raw.

A shadow shot over him. He looked up. Buzzards had gathered, wheeled above him, descended in slow spirals.

He crawled into the rind of shade beneath the horse. The birds came down, landed, feasted, flapped off screaming when he moved, came back. He fought off sleep, fought off the strong, curved beaks that snapped at his bloodied body.

With night he left the place. In the darkness he stumbled, lost direction, fell again and again. At last he crawled.

He put out a hand, brought it down on nothing, pitched forward, kept going. It was a cliff face. He had not seen it. He rolled, slid, tumbled, bounced across rocks. Then he fell clear.

The splash shocked him. Water closed over his head. Current caught him, swirled him, too strong to fight. His feet could find no bottom. His head broke the surface. He breathed, was pulled under again, swept in a circle. Then he was carried against a bar, rolled onto sand.

He crawled, got his trunk clear of the tugging current. There he slept.

Chapter SEVEN

Sun rising over the edge of the cut stabbed his eyes. He waked. Awareness came slowly. He lay on wet sand, his legs awash. He was in a canyon with sheer walls, twenty feet deep. The stream that sluiced through it eddied here, caught behind a rock fall. In the middle of the badlands, a stream. He was alive.

He rolled full into the water, soaked his head, felt its cold bite against his blistered skin. The pumice in his clothes was mud now, abrasive grit. He crawled to the bank, stripped, scrubbed the clothes, and washed his feet with special care. A man afoot out here had need to care for his feet.

He remembered the night of wandering. He had, he thought, been delirious. He did not know where he was, how far it was to Spokane. Sidney Blood was in Spokane. Johno Wade was headed for Spokane. With Hope. They would meet Blood, collect money for their information, and Blood would change his plan. Lassiter must be in a place to learn what the change was.

A waterfall filled the upper canyon. He could not climb

the walls here. That left him one way to go. He started downstream. Swam the eddy, climbed across the rock fall, and found the water shallower beyond.

Where he could, he walked, fought the strong pull of the current. At the deeper pools he floated, conserved his strength, let himself be carried around the whorls to the lower channel.

The canyon twisted, turned back upon itself, and coiled through the land five miles to cover two. He was in water all the way. Cold water. But the air was like an oven. He found a shelf, a narrow shell of rock jutting out, undercut by water erosion. He climbed on it, rested his numb legs.

Swift movement below caught his eye. A trout swept in, stopped beneath the ledge, and hung there. Lassiter eased his hand down, broke the surface without rippling it, curled his fingers beneath the fish, lifted them gently, caressed the soft belly. Like underwater grasses waving against it. Without forewarning he closed his hand, thumb and forefinger in the gills, pulled the suddenly galvanized fish up. He had laughed when the old Klamouth had told him the trick. Silently he apologized.

Raw, the fish tasted better than the horse meat had. He ate it all while his legs thawed. Then he went on.

He slept that night on a sharp nest of rocks above water line. The character of the canyon had not changed. He could not get out except by following it. He did not know how far it ran, what lay ahead, how long he would be trapped in it. If it were too long, Sidney Blood's treasure train could roll unchallenged across the plains. It was not a thought he liked.

The second day was like the first, but without a fish. He broiled and froze, walked and swam, filled his belly with water only. His senses dulled.

The sound grew slowly. He was not aware of it until a

kingfisher flashed by, screaming and he caught the background roar. He went toward it. There was no place else to go. He floated through a deep pool, around a bend, heard the heightened crash of water. His speed increased. He was swept toward rapids. He caught at a rock at the head of white water, clung there.

Below him the stream bucked and plunged, broke against slick black rocks, threw spray and spume that raised a watery veil. He had no choice. If he stayed where he was he would soon starve.

He let go of the rock.

He was caught, flung down a smooth sluice, tumbled under pounding water, cast up. He snatched breath, went under again, rolled, slammed against stone. He did not fight. He could not. He was moving too fast. He was giddy, reeling, unable to tell up from down. Then near drowning, he was sucked beneath branches that dragged in the water, whipped by them. Before he could catch at them he was past.

Suddenly the tumult was over. He was in still water, drifting toward a shore. He brushed it, reached for it. His hand closed on grass. It held. His arm shook as he put tension on it. His feet hit solid bottom. He thrust up. His knees buckled, but he fell forward on dry ground.

He waited until he could move, then rolled to look around. The canyon was behind him, a split in a cliff face. Below him was a rolling land, green grass, trees.

He smelled smoke. He saw its quiet plume rising behind a rounded knoll. He got up. By concentrating on each step, one after another, he could stagger toward it. He left a trail of fresh blood, from his face, his arms, his legs.

It was a log house, solid, in good repair, flanked by out-buildings and a strong corral. There were horses in the corral. The smoke rose from a large stone chimney. The slab door was held closed by a metal latch.

He came against the door, laid his face against it, fought for consciousness, lifted the latch. The door pushed open. He heard a woman shout, then he fell forward into the room. He did not know when he struck the rough plank floor.

It was night when he roused. A lamp burned in the room. He lay in a bed, beneath a blanket. The wool scratched. He was naked, warm, dry. He did not want to move. He turned his head. The room said prosperity but not wealth. In a slat backed chair beside the door a woman sat.

She was tall, angular, past youth. Straight black hair parted exactly in the middle was pulled to a severe bun at the nape of her neck. Her face was long, cheekbones high and prominent as an Indian's. Her mouth was wide, thin, still with practiced control. She sat stiffly, her hands quiet in her lap. She wore a black dress unrelieved by ornament. She saw his movement, stood up, came toward him. This close he noticed the up-cant of her black eyes. A dark life moved in them. She was not pretty, not handsome. But she was compelling. She said, "How did you get here?"

He tried his voice. Tried twice. "Came down the canyon."

The muscles at her temples tightened, drew out the corners of the odd eyes. "I'm surprised you're alive. I wouldn't believe you if I hadn't seen your clothes, your body."

He became conscious of bandages. He moved to sit up. She put a large hand on his bare shoulder, held him back. There was a man's strength in the hand.

"Lie quiet. You need more rest."

She went out, her long stride making the long black skirt cling about her legs. She brought a bowl of soup, rich with chunks of meat, onions, beans, watched as he wolfed it. She was there when sleep claimed him again. She was in the chair when he waked. It was as if time had not passed. But his clothes were laid on the foot of the bed. Washed, ironed, mended. And he felt restored. He looked at the dark, intent eyes.

"When did you do all that?"

"You've slept for two days."

"Two days . . . ?"

He sat up sharply, swung his feet to the floor, looked at her. She stood up but did not leave. He flung the blanket back, dressed under her unwavering watch.

"Your boots," she said, "are in the kitchen." Then she went through the door.

He followed. The boots were beside the stove, the leather warm. They had been softened, worked with tallow, left to steep. He did not thank her. Something in her bearing warned him not to.

The dog got up as they came into the kitchen. It stood taller than the table, big as a calf, a liver grey, short-haired beast. A Great Dane. Lassiter had heard of the breed, had not seen one before. It came stiff legged, head thrust forward, suspicion hard in the light eyes that rolled up at the woman. It put the enormous head against her middle, sniffed at her, turned to regard Lassiter without love.

She said, "All right, Wotan, all right," and to the man, "Go out and walk a little. Look around. I'll get supper."

He had not known it was evening. He had intended to leave at once. He went outside, walked to the corral, looked at the horses there. They were sleek, good animals. He turned away and found that the dog had followed him, stood back from him silent, the eyes steady and unblinking. He could feel its hatred of him.

He ignored it, breathed deep of the fresh, warm air, looked toward the cliff. It loomed black, forbidding, the bleak badlands rising behind it. Down here, abruptly, the land was sweet, abundant. Fruit trees bloomed, pale and soft above the lush grass that spread over rolling ground as far as he could see. There were cattle in the distance, heavy-bodied animals, fine stock. He had never seen a better spread.

When he went back to the house the table was set. For two. The woman brought antelope steak, greens, hot bread. Even if he had not been famished he would have eaten it all. Food like this was rare in his experience.

She sat across from him, watched him openly. Afterward she took him to the main room, waved him to a deep chair beside the fireplace, brought him a pipe and tobacco. He sank back, looking into the flames, finding the tobacco good, relishing the comfort. Across from him the woman took an armless rocker, reached beneath it for the traditional evening work. It was not a sewing basket she brought to her lap. She was braiding a supple lariat. The dog stretched at her side, chin on its forepaws, paws better than half the size of his hand. The eyes never left Lassiter.

He finished the pipe, knocked it out. She rose, brought a tray with brandy and a glass, put it on the polished table beside him, sat down again. She watched him taste the brandy. It was excellent.

"Would you like a job here?"

The words startled him. "What makes you think I haven't got one?"

"You came from the Hole in the Wall."

"I did?"

"You talked in your sleep. About Cassidy."

He was very still. "What did I say?"

She noted his tension. Her lip turned down. "Something about gold. It wasn't clear. You needn't worry, there's no one here to talk to if I wanted to."

He sat forward. "Who runs this ranch?"

"I do. My man was killed. Eight months ago."

A strange dryness in her voice made him ask. "How?"

"By . . . by an animal."

He stood up, made restless by something he did not understand, turned toward the bedroom.

She said, "About the job . . . ?"

"I'll think about it."

He went to bed. He heard the woman stir, heard the kitchen door open, heard her call the huge dog. They went outside. He was almost asleep when the bedroom door opened. There was no light except that from the stars, filtered through the open window. It was enough to show him the tall figure, the white body. She came to the bed, came in beside him.

There was no soft yielding about her. Instead, a cold passion, direct as a blast of wind. She was the aggressor, directing the battle. It was a battle. She took from him. Drained him. Sated herself of him. The sounds from her throat were loud, the deep growls of a straining animal.

Outside, the dog set up a clamor of barks and howls. Apparently it was chained. He heard heavy links rattle, snap taut, heard the scrabble of nails in the big paws against wood, a post, or a wall.

When he was exhausted, when he slept, his nerves were still tense. His need was gone but he was not assuaged.

He waked early, found her eyes open, on him, the dark life in them moving. The wide mouth did not smile.

"You could stay here, you know."

"I've got something to do."

"You could come back. There are over two thousand head of cattle. Over a hundred horses. You could have half."

"Why?"

"The place needs a man."

It was a temptation. To stop moving. To settle here on this benign land. To know plenty, and comfort.

He threw back the cover harshly, climbed across her. She lay on her back. It was the first time he had seen her body. It was strong, taut, flat bellied, more like a sculpture than flesh. The legs were long, well shaped. Down the side of one ran four parallel red streaks, scratches, healed but not yet faded. She rolled, hiding them.

She waited until he had dressed, gone out of the room before she rose. When she came to the kitchen she wore riding clothes and soft boots. Without words she cooked a breakfast.

Afterward she went to a gun case against the wall, took from it a belt and holster. The holster held a Colt.

"You'll need this."

He fastened it around his flat hips, looked toward the rifles in the rack. She went back, brought a Winchester, put it in his hands.

"You'll need a horse. The black in the corral is the best. There's gear in the barn."

He went to the barn, found a good saddle, bridle, carried them to the corral. The Great Dane was chained to a corral post, leaping, lunging against the thick chain. It would kill him if it could break free.

He caught up the black, saddled it, mounted, rode back to the house as the woman came out to the porch. She wore a riding hat, carried another, extended it to him. He found that it fit.

"What's the closest town?"

"Buffalo. Follow the Crazy Woman. The stream. Here, catch."

She tossed something from her hip. He caught a small leather purse heavy with coins. His instinct had read the toss as the drawing of a gun. He saw the gun belted against her side. Suspicion blanked out his surprise at the purse.

"You're riding someplace?"

One corner of the long lips lifted. "I told you not to worry. When you've finished whatever you're doing, come back. I need a man. A strong man."

"I want to know where you're riding."

She looked toward the corral, toward the furious, jealous beast chained there. She looked at it unafraid, as if she knew that when the man was gone it would quiet.

"Wotan and I. We have a ranch to run. I would rather it were you than he."

He touched the hat, turned the black, rode through the scented orchard and deep, sweet grass. It was a ranch to satisfy any man's soul. He knew that he would not see it again.

Chapter EIGHT

Spokane was big, sprawling, raw, busy. The railroad made it a major hub of traffic in the far west. From here were shipped the long lumber trains, the wealth of the great mines scattered through Idaho and Montana, the cattle rounded up and driven to the pens from the high country ranches. The town was constructed of hurriedly raised, unpainted shacks. The main street was a fire trap in dry weather, a muddy wallow in wet. The whole place stank with the acid richness of the crowded cattle, the heavy pitch of new cut wood, the acrid fumes of unmilled ore. The streets, the few board and batten hotels, were crowded by transient visitors. Timber beasts out of the hills. Sawmill men, the girls who lived off them. Travelers headed west toward new land.

Sidney Blood looked down on it from the second-story Wells Fargo office in the company building beside the freight yard. The big web of tracks, the smoke belching, chuffing switch engines, the clanking of couplings and clicking of switch joints made a scene of urgent activity, a racket that spelled big profit for the company.

His blue eyes surveyed it with arrogance. Blood would have been arrogant even without the massive power of the express agency behind him. But he had it, and it was massive. Wells Fargo ruled the west with an iron hand. Broke its competitors. Tracked the outlaws that threatened it across state lines, across borders. The pride of James Hume, head of its secret police, was that his agents never quit, never gave up the trail of those who tried to rob its shipments. There were many of them. Many agents. Many holdup attempts. Many shipments.

The one concerning Blood now was among the most important he had ever handled. He meant to get it safely through. He believed he had it safely arranged.

He stood at the window, methodically worrying over the plans like a dog with a cleaned bone. To be sure. To leave nothing undone.

Through his concentration he heard the door latch. He spun on instinct, reflex snapping his right hand to the gun beneath his armpit. There was security here, but his mind was on robbers.

Two men came in. He dropped the hand. Clyde Turk, special agent assigned permanently to Spokane . . . this was his office. He pushed the man ahead of him. The man stumbled. A bum. A nondescript who hung around the town bars. An informer, picking up scraps of information, and selling them to the company. Wells Fargo did not care where it got its news. It paid spies throughout its empire. To keep that empire safe.

Blood judged the informer. Thirst was a cancer in the sagging belly. He had to have money. Had to have booze. He whined when Turk prompted him.

"A new man in town, looking for Blood. Asked the bartender at the Columbia where to find you. Bartender pretended he didn't know."

"What man?"

The informer shrugged narrow shoulders. "I dunno. Never saw him before."

Turk had crossed to a file, pulled out a sheaf of reward posters, tossed them on the desk.

"See if he's in here."

The man riffled through the papers, stopped at one, stabbed a dirty finger at the heavy face. The poster read, *Johno Wade, wanted, two thousand dollars reward.* Blood looked at the surprised eyes. He would not forget a detail of what he saw in the quick glance.

The Columbia was a dive, at the far edge of town. Sawdust on the floor was thick, filthy, the backbar mirror was cracked. The moose head above it hung at a crazy angle. The room was filled, noisy. The big stranger was still there, at a table, his hand around the neck of a whiskey bottle. He made the bartender nervous. Asking about Blood. Blood could mean trouble. He did not want trouble. It was always expensive. He was more nervous when he saw Clyde Turk's head outside the batwing door.

The stumblebum came in, went to the stranger, talked to him quickly, then came to the bar for his booze. He had money now. The bartender was sour, watching the stranger get up and take his bottle into the rear room. He wished to hell Wells Fargo would make its deals somewhere else. It could give his place a bad name, having the agents around like this. At least they kept out of sight, he was grateful for that.

Sidney Blood, sitting at the table where he could watch both the locked rear door and the one into the bar, kept his hand inside his coat as Johno Wade came in. It could be an ambush. That was why Turk was watching the main room. When you bought information you bought from a type he despised, a dangerous type. And he judged

Wade to be one of these. He had wired the San Francisco office, learned the man's record, could figure no reason for one of the Wild Bunch to seek him out except in treachery for money.

He let Johno get the door shut, edge to the table, lick his lips in a taste of greed. Then he threw it at him.

"Johno Wade. Wanted for murder in Bridge, Montana. Wanted for stage robbery at Woods Landing two years ago. Wanted about everywhere. There's a sheriff in the other room I can call."

There was not, but as a stranger Wade wouldn't know. He watched the surprised eyes go around the room, as if the room had changed into a prison, closing on him. Watched Wade pull his big gun, level it. His lips curled in live contempt.

"Go ahead. Shoot. You won't get out that door."

Wade's tongue wet his lips. He hesitated, then eased the gun back to its place, lifted the whiskey bottle, upended it into his throat. While he was swallowing, Blood shot at him.

"What have you got to sell? How much?"

Johno coughed, spat out liquor. He risked a smile. This sounded better. He tried to bargain.

"I took a chance, coming here. If Cassidy finds out, I'm a dead man."

"Then money wouldn't do you any good, would it? What's your story?"

"It's worth plenty. I'm saving you half a million."

Blood stiffened. It did not show outwardly. There was only one transfer of that size planned. The gold from the Homestead mine. He had hoped the secret had been kept. But it had not. There was a leak. There had been leaks before. He accepted the inevitable. He would pay for the disclosure, if he didn't his sources would dry up. But he could take some pleasure first. He could enjoy tormenting the man before him. He grinned.

"Thanks very much. I know what shipment you mean, and that you're one of Cassidy's gang. I'll be prepared. You can go now."

Johno Wade's mouth fell open. He had meant to ask for ten percent. Too late he saw that he had given what he meant to sell, or part of it. His face turned cunning.

"You don't pay me for that, I don't tell you the rest. I want five percent."

Slowly Blood fished a roll of bills from his pocket.

"What rest?"

"The name of the man who brought the deal to Cassidy."

That would be worth something. Blood expected to hear who the spy was, where the leak was. He peeled off ten hundreds, fanned them on the table.

"Well?"

Wade leaned forward, spread his hands over the bills. He wanted more, but money on the table was worth a lot of dreams. And revenge was what really counted. His grin was wide.

"Goes by the name of Lassiter."

"Lassiter?" The name burst out. Sidney Blood seldom betrayed surprise. He did now. "That's a lie. Lassiter is dead. Burned up in a crib in Orillo. He. . . ."

Cold swept over him. His mind flashed back. He had seen the corpse. But it was past recognition. It was only the gold and diamond belt buckle found with the body that had convinced him. He looked up at Wade. Wade's head was pulled stubbornly into the bull neck.

"That's the name he called himself."

The coldness grew in Blood. He had thought it was finished. Thought he had triumphed over his arch enemy.

He had chased the man for seven years, had had him in jail time and again, had seen him convicted of murder and almost hung. That he had not been guilty of the murder had not mattered, his obsession with finishing the chase had been that deep. And Lassiter had broken that jail, had laughed at him. For seven years Lassiter had laughed at Wells Fargo. And then the fire. And he had not heard of his old enemy since. He had to be dead. But the deep cold would not go away. His voice shook.

"Did you see him? What did he look like?"

Wade was shocked by Blood's reaction. And pleased. "Mister, I've seen plenty of him. It was him broke me out of the Bridge jail."

Blood's voice whipped. "Describe him."

Wade did not have to. He pulled out the dodger with the picture, the one he had taken from Cassidy's cabin.

Even the picture seemed to laugh at Blood. It hypnotized him. It was here to haunt him. Lassiter was haunting him. And Lassiter knew about the gold at the Homestead mine. Lassiter was going for it.

He fought for control. Breathed to the bottom of his big lungs.

"Do you know where he is?"

"Sure. At the Hole in the Wall."

Blood closed his eyes. Bitterness ate at him. He could never take the man out of that stronghold. He could not, but. . . . . He held up the roll of bills.

"You wanted five thousand. I'll give you five thousand."

Wade slavered. He reached. Blood pulled his hand back.

"Get Lassiter out of the Hole where I can reach him. Or kill him. Bring me his head. Take the thousand now, you get four more when I know he's dead."

Wade's cry was animal. He too wanted Lassiter dead. Had never wanted anything as much. But he could not get him away from the Hole. He felt his visions slipping away.

"I can't get to him. I can't go back there myself. He won't come out until that gold moves."

Blood nodded, bitterness in his mouth. "No. He wouldn't. The gold. Wells Fargo gold. That's all the devil wants. That and women."

Wade was slow-witted, but not too slow to make this connection. The idea exploded in him. He hated the thought. His jealousy fought it. But four thousand dollars was a lot of money. And to get Lassiter was worth a sacrifice.

He sounded breathless. "He wants my woman. He fought me to get her."

"Lassiter fought for a woman?" That was new. Blood had never known any woman to be that important to the man. But his hope was tempered. "Where is she now?"

Had he moved, Wade would have strutted. "With me. At the Washington hotel here."

Blood's eyes began to glow. "You beat him? You kept her? Would he come out after her if he heard she was free of you?"

"I'd bet on it."

A low chuckle began far down inside Sidney Blood, grew, belched into a short laugh.

"Can you get the word in to him?"

Wade nodded.

"Then do it. Tell him she'll meet him in Sheridan. I'll have a welcome mat out for him there."

Wade fumbled, cautious. "He's cagey. Maybe he's got a way of knowing whether she's there or not. . . ."

"Then take her there." Blood tossed the roll of bills in his hand, caught it. "You want this, go earn it."

Johno Wade stood a moment longer, splay-legged, emptying the whiskey bottle. Then he dropped it, heaved around, stamped through the door.

Clyde Turk watched the outlaw come down the long room, pass him, slap out to the street. He idled after him. Johno looked back a time or two, did not notice Turk. The sidewalk was crowded, the road filled with wagons. Toward the edge of town Turk lagged back two blocks, saw Wade turn in at the Washington hotel. The special agent did not increase his pace. The hotel clerk worked for Wells Fargo, and kept Turk informed on the comings and goings of guests.

Wade was out of sight when Turk came in, glanced up the stairs.

"Which room?"

"Twenty-one empty?"

The clerk shook his head.

"Twenty-three?"

The clerk was already handing Turk the key. Turk climbed the stairs, surprisingly light footed. His boots made no sound on the bare treads. The upper hall was dim, the air smell hot and dirty. The air in twenty-three was closer yet. Turk did not notice it. He was too familiar with the hotel, with hotels all across the west. The rooms were all alike, narrow cells, sagging beds, a single window, warped washstand, chipped bowl and pitcher, wide glass transom above the door.

Because of the transom Turk would have preferred twenty-one. By standing on a chair he could have looked across the hall, into twenty-two. As it was, he was next door to Wade. However, the wall between was only one thickness of board pasted over with cloth. Not soundproof. He could hear Wade clearly, hear the woman's answers, visualize the scene by the tones.

Wade sounded in a good humor, his gutteral laugh loud. "Climb out of that hay, I tell you. Quit gawping at me so stupid. We got it made, I tell you. Money. A thousand here. A lot more coming."

He must have showed the bills. The bed springs creaked suddenly. The woman must have sat up. Her words came sharp, indrawn.

"For what, Johno?"

"For that bastard boy friend of yours. For Lassiter."

"Oh." It was a whimper.

Wade mimicked her. "Oh. Yes. Blood wants him, four thousand dollars worth. We're gonna collect."

She sounded hurried. "You can't, Johno. You can't go back to the Hole."

His laugh was a shrill, drunken giggle. "Girl, I don't have to. I just send in word you're waiting for him in Sheridan. Then we just sit and watch him come busting down there after you."

Turk heard the deep groaning protest, then the cry of pain, the echo of the slaps, Johno's voice.

"You don't learn, do you baby? Don't you know who you belong to yet?"

"To you, Johno. But make me want to. Please. Let him alone."

"Why damn you! I guess I got to knock him out of your system."

Clyde Turk pursed his lips, wrinkled his face at the sounds of the beating, the muted, sharply cut off cries. Then the room was still for a moment. Then Wade's voice again, breathless.

"Now you do what I say. Take this paper and pencil.

Write your boy a letter that you'll meet him in Sheridan. Don't do it and I'll break your arm."

There was more silence. Then,

"Now address it. Jim Dorne, post office, Mayworth, Wyoming." The tone changed, Wade sounding incongruously. "Dorne handles Cassidy's business outside. He'll get this in. I'm going out now and mail it. You stay here, patch yourself up, get some sleep. Tomorrow you and me start for Sheridan."

Turk boggled. He thought he heard a kiss through the wall. He waited. The door opened, closed, Wade's footsteps thumped down the stairs. Turk gave him time, went down, dropped the key at the desk, went on to the street.

Two of his men were squatted against the front wall, smoking, apparently with nothing on their minds beyond idle gossip. He begged a light, spoke as he bent for it.

"Watch for the girl. Bob, take the back. If she goes out, stay with her. If she makes a break, bring her back." He went on.

Chapter NINE

Hope lay crosswise on the bed, on her face, legs hanging off one side, arms stuck out at the other. Hurt, despair numbed her. She could not say what it was she felt for Lassiter, something that had made her try to protect him. She did know that she could not stand against Johno Wade.

She heard the door open, did not move, did not wonder that Wade was back so soon.

"Hope. Come on."

She convulsed, rolled, doubled to sit up, gaped.

"Lassiter."

He came forward, offered his hand to pull her up. "Let's go, Hope."

"I can't. Johno told me to stay here."

"Loud, isn't he. I heard him across the hall. On your feet now."

He took her arms, lifted her, steered her to the window. He stepped to the shed roof outside, reached back and pulled her through. She did not resist, but did not help. She was like putty. He led her toward the roof edge.

A man turned the corner below, his eyes up. He stopped, yelled, and slapped for the gun at his hip.

Lassiter jumped. His feet struck the chest, knocked the man down, cracked a rib. Lassiter caught his balance, took the man's gun, and slashed it across his head. The man lay still.

Lassiter watched the alley entrance, ready. The single shout brought no help. When he was sure he stood under the eaves, called up softly.

"Come on, Hope. Sit on the edge and slide down. I'll catch you."

She came, with no volition of her own. He swung her to the ground, held her arm, ran with her across the alley, between two buildings, turned in at the livery where he had left the horses.

He flung a coin at the barn man, hoisted the girl into the saddle, stepped to his own, quirted her horse, drove it down the side street toward the open river valley beyond. He pulled alongside her, held the girl from falling, drove the horses to their utmost for five miles, stopped at the crest of a rock shoulder.

"You going to be able to ride?"

She was bruised, disheveled, her hair hanging wild, but the hard ride had brought some life back to her. She nodded. He turned to study the backtrack. The sun had dropped behind the western hills, did not blind him now. Far off there was dust, moving fast toward them.

"Company coming," he said. "Time to go."

Five miles back, on the plain, Sidney Blood rode at the head of twenty men. Cold fury rode with him. He had been caught aghast when Turk's wounded guard was hauled into the Wells Fargo office. He had raged. At himself, not at the men. He should have known Lassiter would come into Spokane after the woman. It was in the old pattern. The unexpected. Always, the unexpected. And he never learned. But now Lassiter was out of the Hole, near by, handicapped by the girl. There was time to run him down.

For company he had an experienced crew, with two Indian trackers. And a new recruit as furious as himself. Johno Wade. Wade wanted to race out hell-for-leather. Blood put him under his gun to hold him back. There was nothing to gain by exhausting all of the horses. Blood would take them out together, split the company into sections, send one ahead to drive Lassiter to keep a top pace. Bring up the others, send them on in relays. He would keep Lassiter running until the man's horses dropped.

From his point of vantage Lassiter saw the dust separate. He read the pattern, set his course. He did not hurry. He knew exactly where he was going. How to get there. And he had no intention of playing Blood's game. He headed for the north shore of Coeur d'Alene lake, the wilderness beyond. Unexplored, towering, sharp timbered ridges, narrow gorges, rushing streams. If he couldn't lose Blood in the country it was time to quit.

He held his horses to a light trot. Let them slow on the upgrades, rested them at the top of each ridge.

The girl rode ahead, in panic. Lassiter herded her horse, she did not control it. The silent man behind her was crazy. Nobody she had known played with danger the way he did: put himself in jeopardy so carelessly. Broke Johno out of jail. Rode as a stranger into the Hole. Came right into Spokane when he knew Johno was talking to Blood. Took her away under the noses of Johno and Wells Fargo. Even if he could dodge Johno, he was bringing the whole power of Wells Fargo down after him.

She had no courage. She could never stand against the

tricks life had played on her. Like a leaf tossed about by the wind. Wade's anger reached out, terrified her. The grim men, like bloodhounds baying behind paralyzed her. She felt naked to a winter blast. Alone. With no help. Nothing to save them but Lassiter's guns. Lassiter's wits. Guns, killing, made her sick. Worst of all, she did not want to die.

Lassiter was not afraid of death. Long back he had met it, danced with it, courted it. They were engaged. He belonged to her. One day the black lady would claim him. Until then he was free. The black lady. It made him think of the dark shadowed woman on the Crazy Woman creek. He still rode her black horse. It was good. Better than the bay he had brought for Hope. But that was a good animal too.

He used both with respect, kept his balanced pace. Let Blood's relays gain. But not catch up.

Darkness came. He rode through it, climbed into heavy timber. Watching the skyline, he found what he looked for. The gap of a side trail. He passed it a hundred yards, called to the girl. They turned off into the black timber.

A good tracker could find their trail. But not in darkness. The needles made a silent sponge underfoot. He made a wide swing, came back to the side trail a quarter of a mile from where it cut off from the main way. The track was a straight, steep rise below and above. An old lumbering skid. In winter the logs cut high in the mountain were dragged to the skid, sent shooting down the snow slope, loaded on wagons at the bottom, hauled to the mill.

He pulled the girl from the saddle, sat her on the ground to rest, waited, listened. Blood's crew would take one of two courses. They would either drive by on the wagon road or camp at the base of the skid. Trying to hunt down their prey across this forested mountain face at night would be a fool's waste of energy. Sidney Blood was not a fool.

He heard the first relay, the jingle of harness. It swept by below him, faded beyond the muffling trees. He waited. Another came up, and went on. Four of them, a mile apart.

The last one stopped, wheeled. Lassiter could picture the conference. That would be Blood, making his decision. Lassiter guessed what it would be. His smile broke when he was proved right. The harness jingled again. The horses ran by.

He mounted the girl, turned up the skid. Up, up, over the saddle. Rested there. Put the horses down the far side. Now there was a quarter moon. Below them it reflected a shimmer off water, showed the faint shadow of the lake shore. He did not drop that far, kept to the height.

At daylight he called a halt, made coffee, rested the horses for two hours. He buried his fire then wet it well. Left to itself it would eat underground, feed on the pitch in the soil, become a live, burning serpent, surface in some distant spot, blaze into forest fire. He waked the girl. She was pale now, tired.

They moved ahead. They crossed rocky ground now, shoulders of basalt angling down to the lake, bald, dry rock. Three miles of that. Then a side draw opened. Water sluiced over the rock planes in a sheet. He turned upgrade, ankle deep. No chipping, no scar left by a shod hoof could be seen beneath the fast running water. But it was slippery. Dangerous going. He took time and care.

They reached the crest, pulled off to dry ground, camped. The horses stood splay legged, head down, near exhaustion. The girl sank to lie full length. He brought water, lifted her head, held the cup to her lips, forced her to drink.

"Sleep now. There's a long way yet."

She coughed, whispered. "Where are we going?"

"Where they won't expect us."

"Where do they expect us?"

He smiled. "They headed for the Hole. When it's dark we'll circle back west."

She slept without stirring. Confident that he had lost pursuit, he backtracked to be certain. He found no sign, no movement other than a deer, some small animals belonging to the vast, silent land.

Three nights later they rode up the grade below the Homestead mine. A hundred miles north of the Hole in the Wall. A hundred miles from the hidden line of men Sidney Blood had flung out to intercept them.

The Homestead was a gravel operation. One of the biggest gold mines in the country. The open pit stretched two miles across. For twenty years men, like ants, had worked it down, scooping out the rich sands. Twenty-four hours a day. By night flaming torches fought back the dark. Donkey engines raised the scoops, like feeding dinosaurs, dumped them into cars. Laboring engines hauled the cars up from pit to surface. The ore was washed. The gold was molded into bars on the property, stacked in the stout log storehouse, held for shipments in large lots. For the same twenty years men had fought for ownership of the mine. In the recent fight the store had doubled, tripled, to the horde that Sidney Blood must soon ship safely east.

Lassiter saw the red glow of the torches from the distance. He detoured the pit, kept well clear of the mill, the cluster of mine buildings. He took the private road to the big house alone on the shelf, high above the din of the mine. It was after midnight. The house, the shelf were dark.

He left the girl mounted beside the corral, left his horse, walked around the house, rattled the front door. Boyd Arkland was a heavy sleeper. Lassiter gave up knocking, threw a rock through the open upper window, heard it strike wood, loud.

Light bloomed in the room. Arkland's head, in nightcap, stuck out of the window. His voice was nervous.

"Who's there?"

"Lassiter."

There was a choked squawk. The head disappeared. The light came down stairs. The door bolt was drawn. Lassiter pushed the plank inward, walked through. Arkland was barefoot, grotesque in a long nightshirt. He bolted the door, scuttled to the living room, pulled heavy drapes. The lamp in his hand shook.

"You're out of your mind, coming here. If Blood should see you . . ."

"Blood's a long way back, watching at a rathole."

Fear oozed from the mine manager. He bleated. "If he ever found out I'd . . . I'd . . ."

"Spilled the beans to me?"

Lassiter's contempt came through his voice. He despised a sneak. Arkland was a sneak. Mine manager here for ten years under the old control. Wells Fargo had won the court battle, Arkland was due to lose his job. In peevish bitterness he had betrayed his trust to Lassiter.

"Don't wet yourself. Sidney Blood is too busy right now trying to waylay me somewhere else to wedge in the idea I might be here. When he doesn't catch me he's going to be worried over how to out-fox me."

Arkland went pale. "He doesn't know about us?"

"He knows I know the gold is slated to go out on the Oriental Express."

"How did he find out?" It was a whisper.

"I sent him word."

The nightshirt trembled. Arkland danced as if on hot coals. "Get away from me. Get out. I won't have another thing to do with it."

"You will. Unless you want me to send him the letter you wrote to me."

Arkland collapsed to a chair beside the table, nearly dropped the lamp, clattered it to the table, traded it for a whiskey bottle there, swallowed, cried with his mouth still full.

"Why? Why? What are you trying to do to me?"

"You I don't care about. I'm trying to make sure that Sidney outsmarts himself. If he sends that gold out on the Express with a coach load of armed guards in front and behind I'd need an army to get to it. I haven't got an army."

Arkland was miserable. "You knew that was the plan when I first told you about it."

"I did. Now I'm trying to change the arrangement. If you want to keep your skin, listen. Listen good. Blood now knows I mean to hold up the train. He'll make the shipment another way. Make him a suggestion, that he ship it in a cattle train, on the floor of a car, covered with straw, a car filled with cows."

Arkland drank again. Lassiter took his bottle, shook the bony shoulder.

"Pay attention. Suggest that he put enough guards on the Express to shoot up anybody who stops it, send it out with the cattle train behind it, and a Special with guards behind that. I want him to feel nice and secure."

The manager looked up, stupid. "He'd murder you . . ."

"I mean him to think so."

"But what about me? If you hit a train like that he'll know I . . ."

78

"By then you'll be in Canada. You'd better be in Canada. I'll send a gold bar up to you. For a keepsake."

He leaned down, took the man's narrow face in his hand, held it, held the weak eyes hypnotically.

"Make it good, Arkland. And when you know what Blood will really do, wire me at the Wyoming Hotel in Casper. Send it to Cliff Jones. You know the code."

He left the man, left the house, went back into the night. It was a lovely, cool, star filled night. He enjoyed riding through such a night.

Hope wanted to know where they were going next. He did not tell her they were going to the Hole.

Chapter TEN

Sidney Blood had the canyon entrance to the Hole in the Wall in his sight. He had a stakeout posted, hidden, all around it. He had missed Lassiter on the trail, but if he was working with Cassidy he would surely come back here. Blood meant to waylay him as he tried to ride in.

Lassiter outwaited Blood. Camped on a ridge well back from the lead-in valley, he was in no hurry. It had taken some time for him to locate each of the Wells Fargo men. Now he watched them at leisure. While Blood was here he would not be busy getting his shipment shaped up.

He waited four days. For Hope they were the best days in her memory. She blanked out the period of terror in Spokane. She had spent her life blanking out her yesterdays, living the day, not looking to tomorrow. For her there had been no tomorrows. So, now, she put away the thought of this respite ending. It was enough to be here with Lassiter. With him everything seemed possible. Whatever he had told her he would do, he had done. She began to believe . . . believe in the mysterious money he talked about . . . believe that some day soon she could be free of people like Johno Wade.

Micronite filter.
Mild, smooth taste.
For all the right reasons.
Kent.

America's quality cigarette.
King Size or Deluxe 100's.

Micronite filter.
Mild, smooth taste.
For all the right reasons.
Kent.

© Lorillard 1972

Regular or Menthol.

Kings: 17 mg. "tar,"
1.1 mg. nicotine;
100's: 19 mg. "tar,"
1.3 mg. nicotine;
Menthol: 19 mg. "tar,"
1.3 mg. nicotine
av. per cigarette,
FTC Report Aug. '72.

Warning: The Surgeon General Has Determined That Cigarette Smoking Is Dangerous to Your Health.

She even began to accept the return to the Hole. She had nearly died when he told her about that. To deliberately go back under Cassidy's domination was unthinkable. She had argued it wildly to Lassiter. He had laughed at her, promised her safety. And even this she believed.

On the fifth day Blood gave up, pulled out. Lassiter beckoned Hope up to the lookout to watch them ride, toward Bridge.

It was late afternoon. After dark he left the girl, dropped off the ridge. He thought his count of Blood's men was right. He meant to make sure. He went to the deserted camp, from it followed each of the paths worn to the points from which they had watched for him. By daylight he knew that they had not left a lone man in ambush.

On the ridge the girl was asleep. He saddled her horse, cooked coffee and fried meat over a smokeless fire, then waked her. He saw her nervousness return as he made ready to ride. He ignored it. It could not be helped.

They rode slowly, openly. The sentry's bullet kicked up dust in the trail ahead. Lassiter pulled up, cupped his hands at his mouth, shouted.

"Tell Cassidy it's Lassiter."

They waited in the sun for an hour. The girl drooped under her strain. She trembled when two men rode down toward them, shriveled visibly when they took Lassiter's guns, tied his hands. She visualized both of them being executed, standing in the grass before the store, the camp gathered to see and take warning.

Cassidy indeed waited on the store porch, his gun on Lassiter. Without words he signaled. Lassiter was cut free. He was handed a gun by a man who ran quickly out of range. He did not keep it. He tossed it to the ground.

Cassidy's eyes were hot. "Get down. Pick it up. I don't shoot an unarmed man."

81

Lassiter did not get down. "Armed or unarmed, shoot me and it costs you half a million. What's sticking in your craw?"

Cassidy's gun did not waver. "I told you not to leave here. I don't tolerate disobedience in my men."

"I'm not your man. I told you I wanted the woman back." Lassiter saw Cassidy look at Hope, saw the urge to kill her in the marble eyes. "Touch her and you'll never see that gold." The voice was very soft.

Still Cassidy debated. It was bad for his image to let this go on in front of the camp. And yet . . . He holstered his gun viciously.

"Get her out of my sight."

Lassiter winked at her. "My cabin."

She hurried, pushed her horse. Lassiter did not watch. He eased out of the saddle, stretched his legs.

"You interested in hearing a little news?"

Butch Cassidy knew that he had lost the initiative. Knew that he was not likely to regain it in this public exchange. He cut it off with little grace.

"If it's worth anything. Let's go find out."

He came down from the porch, waggled his dangling hand, walked to his cabin. Lassiter followed. He looked at no one. He wanted no more than Cassidy any lessening of the outlaw's control among these men. They were going to be needed. They would be given temptation enough to defect. A tight rein must be kept on them.

Inside the room, with the door closed, Cassidy spun, let his anger blaze.

"If any other man pulled what you did I'd gut shoot him. Don't ever try to put me down again."

Lassiter's lips thinned out. He sounded thoughtful. "Maybe you're too edgy for this big a job."

"Job . . . job. What job? I'm not even sure there is a

job. All I know is some wild talk from you. How do I know there's that much gold collected?"

"I've seen it. Recently."

The man drew a ragged breath. "All right. Say you have. When does it get shipped?"

"When Sidney Blood is ready."

"How do we know when that is?"

Lassiter sat down, crossed his knee. "You'll live longer if you relax. I came back here to talk plans. Lay out what we have to do. You want to listen or argue?"

Cassidy still hesitated, finally dropped to a chair. His voice was too polite. "I'll be happy to hear anything constructive. Talk."

Lassiter nodded. "It's time for us to move. We go to Casper and wait for a wire."

"Who's we?"

"You, me, and all the men you can corral."

"And when we get the wire, what then?"

"In Casper, we fix on a meeting place, drift out and gather again there. Hit the train, get the gold. Head down the Outlaw Trail. With that big a haul Wells Fargo would chase us clear through Mexico. So we keep going. To South America."

Cassidy, looking at him, was like a cat seeing things invisible to human eyes. He seemed to physically follow the outlined course. He lifted an eyebrow.

"What did you have in mind about the women here?"

"Leave them in the valley. When they get tired of it they'll filter out."

"You know that's going to cause a row with the men."

"I suggest we let them think we're coming back here. Let everybody think that."

"For how long?"

"Until we start down the Trail."

Cassidy's lip curled. "And you think that crowd will stand still for going off without their broads?"

Lassiter kept his patience. "I thought you were a leader? Thought they listened to you. Wait until they've got their hands on the gold, then tell them. They can send back for the women they want. But remind them there are a lot of fresh ones in Mexico. You won't have too much trouble."

"No. I guess not. When you think of it that way." The hazel eyes narrowed. "But what kind of a damn fool are you? You want one special woman bad enough to walk straight into Wells Fargo's front yard to get her. Then you say leave her here."

"I didn't say forever. I'll send word for her to meet me."

The outlaw's laugh was ribald. "And you think she'd come? First she's Johno's, then she's yours. You think somebody else won't pick her off as soon as you're out of sight?"

"She'll come. Now get your mind off women and let's get down to cases. And keep all of this between you and me."

They rode that night. Fifty men behind Lassiter and Cassidy. Outside the valley they separated, drifted into Casper by twos, threes. In the saloons of the town none of them recognized another.

They waited three days. The wire to Cliff Jones came.

"Mama arriving Thursday evening. Cattle shipped as planned." It was not signed.

Lassiter led the Wild Bunch north. Toward their biggest strike. Their last.

Chapter ELEVEN

Events out of the ordinary were happening at places far distant from each other.

At Bad Mountain the night station agent, Bud Hughes, listened to the clatter of the telegraph instrument, wrote down the orders. They confused him. Brought his isolation sharply to his mind. The Oriental Express, crack train from Puget Sound to the East, was due at its normal seven-ten. What wasn't normal was the mixed freight, Number Ten, behind the Express, to be given through clearance all the way to St. Paul. And half an hour behind the freight a Special had the same prerogative. For these three trains all Westbound traffic was to be held off the main line.

Bud Hughes swore. Outside, rain spattered against the bay windows. The platform boards glistened with wet. The yard lights swelled, bloomed behind the wet curtain. It was cold for June. Up here they said if you don't like the weather, wait fifteen minutes. He was tired of waiting. He hated Bad Mountain, longed to go back to Chicago. He was alone here, cut off from knowing anything that was going on in the world. All he heard was what came over the wire, through the little box in front of him, through the clicking key.

Now it was spitting out his call letters again. He opened the key, took down this new unprecedented message. Stop the Oriental at Bad Mountain. The Express never stopped here. He looked up at the grimy wall clock. In only five minutes the proud train would come thundering through the yards. He had to hurry. Had to go out in the damn rain. Had to set the board.

Far away in the hub of Spokane another night dispatcher drowsed at his post. The sudden clatter of his instrument waked him. Then shocked him. He heard the order to stop the Oriental Express at Bad Mountain. No one but he had the authority to give that order. Nobody in the whole system.

He jumped at the key, pounded it, beat out the Bad Mountain call signal, followed it with *Acknowledge, Acknowledge*. He didn't have to watch the key. His eyes nailed on the desk clock before him. Seven-six. At seventen the Express would slam through Bad Mountain.

One mile west of Bad Mountain a man in wet clothes climbed down a telegraph pole carrying a jumper and a portable key. He was grinning. He had just sent the order to stop the Express. Then he had cut the wire short of the insulator. The line now hung to the ground. He ran along it, climbed the next pole, cut the full section away, climbed down. He was rolling up the section when the clicking in the rails told him the train was coming. He dropped into the brush beyond the right of way, stayed there until the cars rattled by. Then he walked to his horse, looped the wire over his saddle horn, rode out through the driving rain. It would take longer to replace a full section than merely to repair a break.

In Spokane the dispatcher was losing his mind. His finger on the key was light, frantic, repeating the Bad Mountain signal, repeating, repeating. He got no response. He followed the clock. Ten after seven. Eleven after seven. Twelve after seven. Too late now, whatever was happening. He sent a call boy with a message to repair. Either Hughes at Bad Mountain was not at his post or the line was broken.

Hughes was not at his post. He had scrambled to set the board, the lights, against the oncoming Express. Now he stood in the rain on the platform, waiting.

Eli Sommers was engineer. Had been engineer of the Express since the train was inaugurated four years ago. He knew all about the huge locomotive. But he had nothing to say about the makeup of the cars snaking behind. And nobody had told him about the gold shipment. He knew it was a miserable night, a strong east wind pelting rain in his face, and that he had to sit there and take it, keep his head poked out the side window of the cab. He didn't want to run headlong into some stupid cow maybe wandered on the track. He knew that in a minute or two the lights of Bad Mountain would rise at him out of the night, flash past.

Across the cab the fireman was also peering out, watching for obstructions from his side. Both men saw the signal ahead go red. The fireman shouted a warning. Sommers hit the brakes. The shout blended with the squeal of metal. Sommers cursed Seattle. The schedule the men there set up was tight. Every minute counted. An unexpected stop at Bad Mountain would have them running late.

Back in one of the through sleepers Abe Calhoun, the

conductor stood by the washroom talking to the porter. He set himself against the first pull of the brakes, glanced at the sluicing windows, pulled his silver turnip watch, read seven-eight.

"Bad Mountain."

He said it aloud, idly. He knew every town, every stop on the line, the entire timetable of the Express, by heart. He was inordinately fond of his train. The best in the west. Felt every throb and shudder like a heartbeat. Sommers, he felt, was touching the brakes, slowing her over the yard switches. He was startled that the braking continued, speed kept dropping. He turned, pulled open the door, went out to the platform. Wind, rain, cinders rushed around him. He went down the open steps between the cars, caught the handrail, leaned out. The station lights showed ahead. He saw the board set against them. No doubt now that they were going to stop.

They would run late. That was bad. It was his personal boast that only once had the Express come into St. Paul late. That time a snow avalanche had buried the tracks in Painter Canyon. The weather was bad enough tonight. A river ran off the stiff bill of his unifrom cap. But rain wouldn't account for this break in schedule.

He worried. He'd been uneasy ever since Spokane, since they changed the regular makeup of cars. Now they hauled three extras, hooked just behind the tender, ahead of the usual dozen sleepers. The one in the middle was a baggage car. Its doors had been barred even before the train was made up. He didn't know what it carried. The other two were coaches jammed with men. His orders were not to collect tickets in either. But he had looked through the glass window of the one ahead of the sleepers, had been shocked at the arsenal of rifles in the racks over the seats.

Something was going on on his train that he did not

know about it, and Abe Calhoun resented it. He wondered if this unscheduled stop had anything to do with the armed men.

In the forward armed coach Sidney Blood wondered the same thing, but not in total ignorance. He stood up, shouted down the car.

"Get ready. Pull those blinds down. Don't anyone raise them or shoot until I say to."

The blinds ran down as if they were one. This was a picked crew, brought in from all over the west. Sidney Blood approved the quick response, the way the men reached for rifles, checked the action. Not a railroad man, Blood had still ridden this right of way back and forth enough to feel he knew every dip and lurch. He knew this was Bad Mountain. Not Painter Canyon.

Painter Canyon was twenty-five miles yet. Rough miles. A long, laborious grade to climb that took its toll of speed. They would not use brakes going into Painter Canyon. But maybe Lassiter and Cassidy were not going to wait to hit them there, where the train would be almost at a standstill. This might be the hit. At Bad Mountain.

He was already moving, pulling open the door, bucking the wind on the platform. The conductor looked over his shoulder. He did not know Blood.

"Better go back inside. We don't stop here."

"We are stopping." Blood put his head back in the coach, gave his order, felt for the gun under his arm. Outside he saw the platform slide past. He dropped off the train. The engine stopped even with the station. Steam leaked from around the cylinders, rose in a white cloud through the rain, the spreading fog. The coach lights were dark now. The windows went up. From them forty rifles covered both sides of the train. The same would be true in the second coach. Clyde Turk had charge there. A steady man, Turk.

The conductor was hot footing it toward the lighted station. He was not expecting a holdup. Blood was. He stayed in the shadow of the stopped train, his eyes on the foggy shadows of the yard. Nothing moved there to bother him.

The engineer now ran toward the station. The station agent came out, waving a sheaf of orders in his hand. Both train men were shouting about their right of way, about being stopped. The agent shook a flimsy paper at them. Blood ran toward them, snatched at the message. Read it.

MEET WESTBOUND PAINTER SIDING EMERGENCY GIVE RIGHT OF WAY.

Abe Calhoun swore a protest, saw the gun in Blood's hand, choked.

Blood looked at the agent. "When did you get this?"

"Five minutes ago . . ."

"Check with the dispatcher?"

"No . . ."

"Check now."

Nobody argued with Blood's order. They ran into the station. But Hughes hit the key. Found it dead. He wasn't alone now. But he liked this less than loneliness. He pounded the key as if he could bring the instrument to life by sheer physical force. Nothing happened.

The conductor sounded uncertain. "The storm . . .?" He did not really believe it.

Breath rushed out of Sidney Blood. "Storm hell. The wires are cut."

The three looked at him again, at the gun he held carelessly. Hughes bristled.

"Who the hell are you?"

"Special agent. Wells Fargo."

For the conductor things began to fall into place. The unexplained extra cars. The armed men. He looked wise.

"So we're carrying a shipment."

Blood did not correct him. The man could be one of Cassidy's bunch. The engineer, the station agent could be. The railroad had found other employees in the outlaw's pay.

Well, the first play had been made. Cut off here in the mountains they might as well be on the moon. The Talking Wire, as the Indians called it, was dead. There was no quick communication. Blood was grimly satisfied. He did not show it. He told Hughes,

"Route out a crew, send it both ways. Find the break and fix it."

They had lost seven minutes now. The cattle train with the gold was bearing down on them. Twenty-three minutes behind now. Too close for comfort.

"Let's roll." He touched the engineer's arm, ran to the locomotive.

The conductor, responsibility for his train riding him, panted up, shouted at the engineer. "I don't know what's happened, but when you hit Painter Siding we'll have to go in the Hole, wait for the Westbound. We can't take a chance."

That, Blood told himself, was exactly what Cassidy wanted. The train stopped. A sitting duck. Out away from nowhere. It offended him that a handful of renegades thought they could challenge the might of the great Wells Fargo network. They would learn. They would ride into the firepower of Blood's eighty loyal fighters. And at last he would have Lassiter.

"I'm going to ride the engine. Just in case."

He climbed into the cab behind the engineer. The conductor ran back along the cars, shooing the curious passengers back on board, waving signals at the brakemen and porters gathered on the platform. He turned, gave the hi-ball, waited until the long train lurched into movement. Then he scrambled up the steps.

Chapter TWELVE

Five miles east of Bad Mountain a spur track curved away south, toward the collection of shacks called Hemite. Once a week an unglamorous train snuffled down these rails, took supplies in to the ranches, lumber outfits, the trading post. The traffic wasn't enough to keep the iron roadway from rusting.

Where the spur left the main line two riders came out of the fog, swung down. One stood watch, gun in hand. The other used a crowbar on the switch lock. The metal stuck. He grunted, threw his whole weight on the switch bar, forced it over. Then they faded back into the dark brush, waited.

The Oriental Express was due at this point eight minutes later.

Engineer Sommers sulked, his jaws overworking the tobacco cud. He did not appreciate a stranger invading his cab, Wells Fargo or no. He didn't like Blood preempting the fireman's seat and window even though the man wasn't using it, was feeding coal in from the tender. He cursed that the drivers spun, slipped on the wet rails, made their getaway a series of jerks that shuddered down every car. He watched the headlamp spear through the yard, pick every grimy detail. Almost every detail.

It did not spotlight the figure in the scrub brush beyond the yard. Lassiter crouched low, let the engine pass. He rose without hurry, swept his slicker back from his legs, vaulted up the embankment, caught the passing handrail at the back of the tender, anchored his foot on the step. His eyes traced down the train. There was no light. No bulking shadow of anyone leaning out from between cars. He climbed, swung over the open edge, squatted on top of the wet pile of coal. It was dark here, fog wrapping around everything, blotting everything.

The headlight fought to give even a narrow, blunt view of the way ahead. The red glow from the boiler box flamed every time the fireman opened the door to stoke the hungry monster, silhouetted the engineer, hand on the bar, head out to the rain trying to pierce the eddying mist. It picked out the third figure on the fireman's seat, head and shoulders thrust through the window.

Lassiter could not identify that figure. The shoulders were bulky under a black slicker. Then the head came inside, a hand holding a wide brimmed hat sagging with moisture. The face turned toward the engineer. Sidney Blood.

Unexpected luck. Lassiter's eyes glowed. He was out of the light. Even if they looked, his head would appear only a lump of coal.

It was a rough ride. The engineer was pouring it on, making up time to offset the delay at Bad Mountain, the wait for the Westbound in the Painter Siding hole. They made the five miles to Hemite Junction in seven minutes.

They hit the altered switch at sixty-five. Lassiter had a tight hold on the tender box, was braced. The engine tilted, swayed, almost went over. Wheels screamed. Took the turn. The switch did not split. Sommers yelled, hit the brakes. The engine righted. Sidney Blood slammed to the steel floor. The fireman fell on top of him. They fought the tangle, fought to their knees. Blood did not understand.

"What the hell . . . ?"

Sommers' long experience paid off. He was too old a hand to try too fast a stop.

"Some damn fool left the Hemite switch open. We're . . ."

Blood didn't hear the rest. His curses drowned it. He did hear the voice behind them, telling Sommers,

"Just keep going south, engine man."

Before he spun, Blood knew that voice. It made his own a shocked shout.

"Lassiter."

"Evening, Sidney."

The engineer was twisting. The fireman reached for his shovel. Lassiter showed his guns, leaning down from the tender. They turned back to their business.

Blood's shock faded. Pleasure replaced it. Lassiter thought the gold was aboard the Express, had stolen the train. It was a neat job. Blood never discounted Lassiter. But this time. This time Blood would win. Lassiter would run his prize to some selected point on the branch line. Cassidy would be waiting there with a crew. Blood wanted to laugh. They were in for a surprise. He wanted to see Lassiter's face when eighty men cut down on him. Wanted to laugh in that face before the man died. And as a dividend, it was going to mean the end of the Wild Bunch.

Blood could taste the victory. Hear James Hume's congratulating speech. Hume and the Superintendent, Valentine, would have him in the big office at San Francisco. Even Lloyd Tevis, president of the company, would be there. They would present him with an engraved gold watch. They would make over him. But good as that was, he would have his own reward. Lassiter.

He played the game. Made no move. He wanted nothing to set off fireworks until they were all before him. He said to Sommers,

"Do whatever he tells you, engineer. He'll kill you as quick as he breathes."

Sommers threw him a sour look. He hadn't like Blood being in the cab. He liked him less now. A coward. Sommers was proud. That his engine was taken over hurt that pride. Blood and the man with the guns, he would like to tackle both of them. But he had a wife, two kids. He would die in the tackling. It would be useless.

He eased the bar backward. The locomotive picked up speed. "Gimme some steam."

The fireman started to rise. Lassiter said, "Stay where you are."

The man stayed.

"Face forward, Sidney. Ease out that gun under your arm. Toss it overboard."

Blood tossed it overboard. He ached to spin, to shoot, to try to take the man even if it got him killed. But there was more to gain. He choked, forcing control.

The train slid on, losing power, rounded a descending mountain curve. Blood, watching ahead, saw the lantern waving on the hillside, out of the reach of the headlamp.

From the tender Lassiter said. "This will be far enough. Pull her up."

96

The engineer pushed the bar. The train slowed. Sidney Blood strained his eyes, looking for outlaws in the brush. It was hard to wait. But he would give no signal until he was certain they were around the train. The brakes bit on the metal wheels.

The long keening sound covered Lassiter's noise. He slid from the coal, dropped into the cab. Blood did not know it when the gun barrel raked his skull. He fell, lay limp. The fireman saw, began a yell. It cut off as the gun creased him, knocked him again on top of Blood. Lassiter turned on the engineer.

"Cut it off."

Sommers jammed the bar in with impotent fury, spat his cud at Lassiter's feet.

Lassiter ignored it, caught the handrail, said a soft, "Adios," dropped away into the night, lit running, heading toward the lantern.

Back in Clyde Turk's coach the agent had survived the wild pitching as the car left the main tracks, gathered himself together, barked orders for his troop to stand ready. He waited, keyed up to bursting, ran out to the car platform, strained to hear Sidney Blood's signal. His mind froze on Blood's command; he was not to tip their hand before the attack came.

In the first sleeper the conductor waited. He did not know what for. He knew they were sidetracked. He knew something was terribly wrong. When the train slowed enough he swung down the steps, dropped to the ground. A dark shadow flashed past the headlamp glow, a man, jumping from the engine, sprinting out of sight in the dense fog.

Turk saw the lantern, the running figure at the same moment. He waited no longer for Blood. He fired. The shot was a signal. Inside the coach the men let loose a broadside.

Lassiter was still running, bent low. Bullets spattered around him. But they were low. The lantern was doused. The fog played tricks with direction. None of the lead found a mark.

Lassiter made out the shadowed bulk of the horses, came in a rush, made a running mount.

"Let's go."

He swung the horse, cut cross country, back toward the main line, toward Painter Canyon. He knew exactly how far it was.

Off around the bend an explosion rocked the air. Heavy. Then silence again, fog, rain seeming to increase.

"What was that?" The rider at his side sounded jumpy.

Lassiter did not answer. Each man knew only his own narrow assignment. Only Cassidy and Lassiter himself knew the full plan. It was a safety measure they could both agree on.

Back at the train they were working over Sidney Blood, the conductor trying to quiet the frightened passengers. The shooting had stopped. All was quiet except the hiss of rain, wind, steam that still escaped the cylinders.

Blood heard that as he came to. He lay on the wet ground beside the locomotive. He saw Turk bent over him, tried to sit up. His head reeled. It hurt when he shouted.

"Where is he?"

"Where's who?"

"Lassiter, damnit. He was on the tender."

Turk's stomach fell an inch inside. "I had a glimpse of him. He ran out in the brush."

"You didn't get him? You let him get away?" Blood thought his head would explode.

"There was a lantern. We shot up everything between it and the train, enough to wipe out the Sioux nation. But then we heard horses. He must have made it through."

Blood fought to his feet, damning his aching head. "Engineer. Get the hell this thing moving. Back it to the main line." He scrambled again to the cab.

Minutes were lost. Passengers milling on the ground had to be rounded up, got aboard. The gunmen from the coaches were scattered, searching the brush. It took them time to get back. The fireman threw coal, trying to build up the lost pressure. The drivers moved sluggishly, the wheels took hold. The cars clanked, backing into each other. Slow, agonizing.

Blood watched from the window, rigid, willing speed with all his being. They had to get back to the junction before the cattle train passed it, the precious, gold bearing cattle train.

He had been suckered. He knew it now. It galled him that he had been so amused at Lassiter stealing the Express. Hell, the man hadn't wanted the Express, only to get it and the army on it out of the play.

"Faster." It came out a croak. "Move this thing, can't you?"

The engineer grunted, threw him a baleful glare.

In that minute the rear sleeper went off the track. The grinding crash echoed like laughter in the cab.

Blood hit the steel deck again, bounced up, flung himself to the ground. He ran, limping. Turk was outside. The conductor was out. The brakeman had a lantern. They hurried. Gabbling passengers followed.

There had not been too much speed yet. The back wheels were twisted, off the rails. But the car had not tipped over. It hung at a foolish angle. Porters were there, pulling dazed passengers out. None was seriously hurt. But they were loud with blame for the crack railroad train they had trusted.

Those who saw it were suddenly silent. The deep hole, fifty feet across. Where the tracks had been. The right of way had been effectively blown.

Chapter THIRTEEN

Behind the Oriental Express the cattle train was balling through.

Clem Easton was engineer. For eight years he had hauled the monotonous strings of mixed freights east. Never had he known a freight to be given right of way over all the westbound traffic. He did not understand, but he had no imagination. He took his orders, took his turn when his name went up on the call board. He asked no questions. But it did feel good.

His fireman was shriveled, redheaded with a pointed nose. Sullivan. Inquisitive. Always butting into things Easton thought were none of his business. A roundhouse lawyer. Always beefing.

Sullivan hurled coal into the box, slammed the door, glared at the steam gauge, at the crack in the glass face that made it hard to read. Routinely he complained that it should be fixed. It still hadn't been.

He should have climbed to his perch, watched the signal lights. He didn't. He crossed the cab, stood at Easton's side, shouted above the rush of rain, the hurricane sound of the racing train.

"What's so all fired important about these cattle that we gotta rush em through like this? Just tell me that, will you? Just tell me . . ."

Easton pretended not to hear. He wanted to order Sullivan up to his proper post. But that would start an argument. Anything you told Shamus Sullivan started an argument. He eased the throttle a little. They were coming into Bad Mountain.

Ordinarily he would have been sidetracked into the hole, waited there for the Westbound express to thunder by. Easton was torn by his preferences. It was good, having the special clearance. On the other hand there was a girl in the coffee joint across the tracks, black hair, red lips, big breasts. He had never touched the breasts but he wanted to. For a few minutes on each run she could make him forget his flat chested wife.

He saw the switch lamps set for him. Saw the station lights come at him. Belted past the wooden platform with a bare glimpse of the night agent keeping out of the wet in the doorway, watching them slide through. He pulled the whistle cord in salute.

On the platform the agent winced, watched the forty stinking cattle cars pass at a dizzy passenger train speed. With that noise and the shrieking whistle he could not have heard the sounder if it had been working. It wasn't. He had sent out repair crews but apparently they had not yet found the break in the line. He felt utterly helpless, completely divorced now from the outside world. The telegraph had been his only link. Beyond his personal isolation it now struck him that when something went wrong with the line it was like running the railroad blind. The caboose swept by, rocking. Then a second caboose. He stood gaping as silence crept back.

Inside the caboose the freight conductor chewed over the knotty question of the five men there with him. Supposedly they were assigned to care for the cattle. But why were cow pokes so heavily armed? Why were they hauling a second caboose? It was unheard of proceedure. And why did they have this through clearance?

He stood on the open platform, preferring the rain and fog, even the flying cinders, to the uncommunicative company inside. They banged through the Bad Mountain yards, ran on east. Clattered across the rough switch of the junction where the branch track curved off sought toward Hemite. They were really rolling.

The caboose was more than a mile past the Hemite Y when he saw the giant flash above the low hills of Hemite Pass. It was several seconds before the blast sound caught up with them. The cigar butt dropped from his mouth. He had seen electric storms in these mountains, many of them. Had heard their crashing thunder. But never like this. This was more like an explosion, like the right of way over which they had just run had blown up. He shook his head. He was seeing things, hearing things. He had better change his brand of whiskey. Or, desperate thought, he might have to give up whiskey altogether.

Half an hour behind the galloping freight came the Special. With the same through clearance. Two coaches. Each carrying eighty men. Special agents of the Express company, lolling in their seats, weapons stacked in the racks overhead, piled in the aisles. None of them knew what they were doing here. Few of them were acquainted.

They had been garnered from many posts throughout the empire. They obeyed orders.

Doyle Palmer was in command. Forty, hardened by years in the saddle, years riding shotgun on one or another stage line. He respected one man in the world. Sidney Blood. If Blood had told him to open Hell's gates Palmer would lead the attack with his sawed off shotgun.

Palmer sat easy. Relax until you need tight muscles. His cigar rolled like a metronome across his mouth then back. His pale eyes watched the rain ribbons on the window. He was one up on his men. He had been told that one of the cars in the freight ahead carried, beneath a false bottom, gold bars worth a half a million dollars. Quite a prize. And plenty of security for it. Palmer himself did not know which was the treasure car. Only Blood knew that. It had been loaded at the mine, then Blood had had it shifted to a different position in the train.

In spite of himself a ball tightened in his stomach. He did not know when the attack would come. If it would come. Blood was riding the express, expecting it to be the target. But there was always the chance of a leak, that the outlaws had been tipped, that they would pass the Express through Painter Canyon, wait and strike the freight. Blood had anticipated that too. The engineer of the Special had orders to watch for any disturbance ahead, to pull up if he found it, let Palmer's crew come up on them from behind.

That was Sidney Blood's thinking. His thoroughness. Butch Cassidy couldn't have more than fifty, sixty gunmen to throw into this try. Blood had eighty in front, eighty behind and maybe fifteen more on the freight, in the two cabooses and strung along through the cars. They couldn't miss. Palmer smiled, recalling Blood's warning of hope.

"If you can, save Lassiter for me. Don't lose him, but save him for me if you can."

The Special slowed. He tensed. Then he saw the switch lamps, the station lamps flash by, heard the click of iron wheels run over the switch frogs. Bad Mountain. They were dead on time.

Half an hour behind the freight, they were due to pick up speed beyond this town. Close to ten minutes behind going into Painter Canyon. A lot could happen in ten minutes, but they dared not run too tight. On schedule he felt the pace quicken.

He brought out a fresh cigar, rolled it, clipped it precisely. Took his time in lighting it. Appreciating that there was no slightest quiver in his fingers to transmit his tension to the match flame. There was a good twenty minutes left before they began the lift into the pass.

He heard the metal clash, was thrown forward against the next seat. The brakes screamed. The two cars bucked against their couplings. Rocked in opposite directions.

Palmer shoved up, helped by the stab of pain. His teeth had bit through his lip when his chin hit the seat back. He bled like a pig. Overhead the lamps swayed crazily. Other men were bleeding, reeling, collecting their cracked heads, snatching at weapons. Palmer pushed through them, ran for the door. On the platform he found the trainman already outside.

"What the hell?"

The man showed him a scared face, eyes widened on Palmer's gun. He dropped to the ground, not answering. Palmer was on his heels. The gun crew was tumbling out. Palmer saw the engineer scuttle down from the cab, ran toward him with the conductor. Up ahead a red flare burned on either side of the track.

So this was it.

Palmer shouted. "Take cover. Look alive."

He jumped for the cab, climbed, peered down the light beam of the headlamp that fought the rain, the streamers of mist floating through. It gave an eerie, uncertain view. Even so he saw the crater ahead, beyond the flares. The tracks ended there. Twisted metal reached frozen fingers into the air. A hundred feet beyond, the far edge of the hole showed dim, mangled. The right of way had vanished.

Below him the conductor's voice kept bleating. "What happened? What happened?"

Anyone who used his head instead of his lungs could answer that. The roadbed was blown sky high. Palmer dropped close to the man, shook him.

"How far to Painter Canyon?"

The conductor needed time to bring his mind around. "Painter . . .? Oh, twenty miles . . ."

"Where's the closest ranch? Where we can get horses?"

"Huh? Oh. Why, I guess Bad Mountain's closest." Thinking came hard. "Yeah. Bad Mountain. Sure. Must be horses there. They got a livery."

Palmer shouted his men back aboard, swung on the engineer. "Get this thing moving backwards. Fast."

The conductor was not to be rattled. He spat. "Mister, I don't know about that. Maybe somebody behind us. Come on us with no warning . . ."

"Then you're going to see one hell of a train wreck. Move." He held the gun steady under the engineer's nose.

They backed.

It was a night of surprises for Bud Hughes at Bad Mountain. Here came the red lamps on the rear of the Special, backing up the way it had gone such a little while before, stopping beside the platform. Here came the engineer, the conductor and a tall, angry stranger, hell bent into the station. The stranger grabbed his shoulder, shook it.

"Get on the wire. Call Spokane. Call St. Paul. Train holdup at Painter Canyon. Call out every law officer around. Tell them it's Cassidy and the Wild Bunch."

The world finally came in around Bud Hughes. It was no longer something far away.

"Mister. I can't . . ."

Doyle Palmer shook him like a terrier. "Don't tell me what you can't. Get on that key." He shoved. Hughes stumbled, shouted.

"I can't. The wires are down. She's dead."

Palmer caught himself up as if he'd been hit. "How long?"

"Before the Express went through."

Palmer swore lividly. "Did Blood know that?"

"Who? What?"

"Blood. Wells Fargo man on the Express."

"Oh. Yes. Sure. The Express stopped here. I don't know why."

Doyle Palmer groaned aloud, swung to his men, now crowding the doorway.

"Get to the livery. Get every horse you can locate." He spun back to Hughes. "Try that key again."

You had to humor crazy people. He tried. It was still dead.

There weren't enough horses. What there were they rode hard, along the right of way. It was slippery. Treacherous. One animal fell as they crossed the side line that ran to Hemite. It was not hurt. The rider climbed up. They raced on. The Hemite spur curved away slowly, toward the gap. Palmer kept to the main track, pounded toward

107

Painter Canyon. Palmer and seven men. The rest were marooned at Bad Mountain.

The long cattle train snaked east through the night. The grade lifted, coming into Painter Canyon. It cut their speed. In the red cabooses at the rear the agents were restless, fingered their rifles, watched the dark windows. Waited, honed, for the attack.

The engineer strained. The rain was heavier. It was impossible to see beyond the shortened beam of the lamp. He was acutely conscious that the Express was somewhere ahead. If it had been stopped he could overhaul it almost before he would see it.

They crawled to the summit. There was no sign of the Express. It was the ideal place for a holdup. A narrow cut. And the train unable to move as fast as a man's walk. Blood had bet on it. He had a line of men well hidden, along the lip of each side of the cut. The engineer didn't know they were there, couldn't have seen them if he had. The lips were deep in fog.

The engine tipped down. Pulled the treasure freight over the top, into the descending grade. The track followed the canyon, wormed around the tight convolutions. It hung on a narrow rock shelf. On one side the wall was high, perpendicular. On the other it dropped, sharp, to the Painter River. Water raged down the gorge now, fed by the storm. Its noise drowned the racket of the freight. It was no place to go over the side. Others had. It was no place for speed. The engineer rode the brakes. They screamed. The wheels slid somewhat on the wet rails. He prayed. Walked the train down like a woman going down a ladder. He was good.

The grade leveled. The canyon widened. They were out

of it, in the valley on the east side. The engineer breathed deep, eased the speed up. The lights of the Westbound, waiting impatient in the hole for its clearance, brightened the fog. Then the freight was past it, heading out into the flat land. The men in the cabooses, the men in each of the cattle cars, relaxed. They were safe through the danger zone. Butch Cassidy had not struck. The flashing rods drove them three miles out, rushed toward the bridge over the river.

Things changed quickly. The brakes bit. Tight enough that the cars bucked. Down the line men were thrown to the floor. Ahead, the engineer peered at the red glow of the warning flares. He made out the bulking barricade behind them. Beyond that he had a glimpse of the herd of white waves. The bridge was gone. The engine made a steaming stop against the barricade.

Back in the darkness Butch Cassidy quieted his horse. The train made it jumpy. Hand on its neck, Cassidy fired his gun into the air. At the signal fifty rifles grouped along the right of way cut loose at the train.

The shots were aimed high, cracked through the roofs of the cars. Not for humanity's sake. Cassidy had no feeling against killing express guards, they knew their chances when they took their jobs. He did not want the cattle hit. The heavy beasts, dead, would make it harder to unload the cars and find the gold.

He watched confusion boil through the train. From both red cabooses came flashes of wild firing. Wild, because he knew the guards there could see nothing but shrouding fog. He waited, watching a mounted figure ride from his line, running, low in the saddle, hunched to make a smaller target. Watched the arc of sparks from the lighted fuse describe the path of the bundle the man hurled. It dropped under the rear caboose. The dynamite exploded. The car rocked, fell off the tracks, on its side.

The firing had stopped. He could be heard. He yelled. "Come out with your hands up, empty, if you want to live."

They wanted to live. He saw their silhouettes fight out of the car, afire now. Saw the guns thrown away, the hands raised. The figures jumped. Flames climbed, turned the fog crimson, like blood. There would be blood in the car, he guessed. Some guards would not come out.

Chapter FOURTEEN

Lassiter was still a mile off when he heard the explosion wreck the caboose. He knew where he was even if he could see little. He knew the distance. He had timed it, ridden every foot of the path across the mountains. In daylight. Until he knew it by heart. It was harder to follow at night, in the storm. He was making better time than he'd expected. He was taking long chances to make time. The Cassidy man who had held the horses for him on the Hemite cutoff had given up. Refused to take the same chances. Even the reminder of the gold on the freight hadn't tempted him enough to make this ride.

Lassiter was spurred by concern for the gold. He needed to be there. He didn't want Cassidy locating it, loading it, disappearing into the fog with it.

They had not found it when he rode up beside the stalled engine. The search was getting frantic. The fog, still red, the torches with smoke streamers, the yelling confusion made an eerie picture. It reassured him. Backed up against the engine the train crew and Blood's frustrated agents were held in a half circle of torchlight. Lassiter passed them, rode down the train, dodging cattle being rushed off the cars on improvised runways. He saw Cassidy, rode to him, swung to the ground.

The outlaw was quartered away from him. He came around, tight faced. His slicker was open, a gun in his hand. The hazel eyes were flaming. There was too much tension in the man, too much excitement. Lassiter grinned by way of easing it.

"Find it yet?"

The head snapped sideways. "Not in the front cars. We're working down." The mouth thinned suddenly. "You real sure it is on this train?"

Lassiter met the eyes, hid his sudden sinking in the stomach. With Blood you could never be certain. Suppose he had guessed wrong? Suppose Blood's army of agents on the Express was actually to guard the gold, not simply to blast Cassidy's mob into eternity? Suppose the cattle freight was the decoy? Had he out-sharped himself. He sounded very certain.

"It's here. Find it fast. Blood's got a crowd back on the canyon rim and an army in the Express and the Special. As soon as he finds horses this country will be crawling with guns."

Cassidy still held his gun. Lassiter waited, hoped he wouldn't try to use it. It would ruin the play if he had to kill Cassidy. His own derringer was cupped in his palm, under the edge of his slicker.

Cassidy seemed to read his mind, looked down at the gun as if surprised, dropped it into its holster. He dropped one eyelid.

"So let's go find it."

They found it in the last car, the one coupled to a caboose. Both cabooses were burning now, the cattle car just catching. The animals were bawling, terrified, scorching. When the door was slid back they jammed the opening. It made a delay. They were prodded back, let out in single file, jumping, hooking the long horns. Some fell from the ramp, lurched up, bolted after the others tails high, lumbered into the night.

There were canvas buckets in the cars, used to water the animals. Cassidy threw a detail to the river, a bucket line to bring water, douse the smouldering car enough that they could work inside it.

Blood had done a careful job, built a false floor on top of the gold, buried it in straw and cattle dung. The animals could not have dirtied it this much themselves.

They pried up the boards. The fourth one to come loose brought a shout. Men ran forward, stared, tore at the other planks. Row on row of ingots rested there. Each bore the Homestead mark. Each thirty-five pounds, around four thousand eight hundred dollars in every bar.

The men wanted just to look. To dream. None had ever dared dream like this. They had not actually believed through the planning of the robbery that the haul could be this much. The very number of the bars stunned. Two whole bars to each man.

Lassiter nudged Cassidy. "They can drool later. Time's getting short."

Cassidy came out of his own stupor, whipped his order across them. "Move. Damn it, move. Get the pack horses up here. Wells Fargo's snorting down our necks."

The remuda of pack horses, enough to carry the gold and some spares, were fitted with special saddles. Leather pockets sewed on a leather pad that hung across the horse. Three pockets on each side. Six gold bars to each horse.

Two hundred pounds dead weight. Plenty to carry if an animal was to travel any distance. His gang might not have believed in the gold, but Butch Cassidy was ready. Cassidy always prepared before he went into any project.

The animals were led to the door in a line. Lassiter brought up one, in his turn. A machine rhythm was working now. One man lifted a bar, passed it to another who passed it on. When it was handed out through the door Lassiter took it, dropped it into a pocket, reached for another. With the horse loaded he pulled out, made room for the next in line.

The loaded animals were herded away, gathered by twos, so that their milling would not create a quagmire. Lassiter led his aside, quiet, without fuss. Within a hundred yards the fog swallowed him.

He was alone. The grey curtain around him stifled breathing, deadened the swish of the hooves on the soft grass, distorted the noise around the train. He quickened the pace. Rode a quarter of a mile, crossed a low ridge, dropped into a gully, reached the natural cave. Here water had undercut a cottonwood, left the crown of roots dangling over an empty hole. He took two bars from the pockets, wedged them into the mud at the back of the hole, watched the gravy thin soil ooze over them. There were loose stones caught among the roots. He worked them free, filled the empty pockets. The weight was not the same, but the leather bulged out, did not lie flat.

He turned back, watchful, satisfied that the lashing rain had already filled his incoming tracks. In minutes they would be gone. He drifted out of the fog, into a group. If the men there even noticed his coming they would assume he came from the train. But they were too elated, and too miserable under the beat of the storm.

The horse he rode put its butt to the wind. The pack animals did the same, waited hipshot, heads hanging. The horses had no sense of urgency. Lassiter did. Patience was one of his strengths. But patience did not mean foolhardy dalliance.

His life, he knew, was uncertain from this point on. Butch Cassidy had no further need of him. Cassidy had the gold in his hands. And he could find the Outlaw Trail from here blindfold. Sometime soon now Cassidy would try to kill him.

The safe thing to do was to fade out now. Leave the pack horse. Ease into the fog, ride for the Hole. It would be awhile before Cassidy would miss him. Probably not before the crew was assembled, was lining out on the long trail. Cassidy would not want him loose, riding the country knowing as much as he did. But at this particular moment time was too pressing. The outlaw could not afford to waste it in any search. And even Cassidy would not be able to force any of these men to trust the others with the gold while they chased through the hills looking for him on a night like this. That was what he should do.

He did not. He had to be certain where Cassidy would head. That he would follow the plan they had made, start at once for Mexico. Devious as the man was, it was possible that he might try to return to the Hole in the Wall after all.

Lassiter's whole project depended on knowing the answer.

He handed the lead rope of the pack horse to the man nearest him, kneed the black, rode down to Cassidy.

"How much longer are you going to be?"

Cassidy grinned. "You getting nervous? Don't. We're ready now. Already started moving."

Lassiter looked toward the head of the train. The beam of the headlamp was steady, stabbing across the barricade to the wrecked bridge. It cast a feeble light on the ford that ran down the steep river bank. They were supposed to use that ford, take to the water, skirt along the shore where the current would wash out any sign of where they had gone. The trainmen, the agents were to be tied, blindfolded, left in a cattle car where they could not see what direction the Wild Bunch took.

He saw the men in the car, a dark mound. He did not see anyone at the ford or near it. Behind him he heard Cassidy's quick laugh.

"A little change in plan. My idea."

"Back to the Hole?"

"Never mind. You just trail along if you want your quarter split. If not, you can cut out now."

"Why? Why the change?"

"To teach you a little lesson, friend. You've been swinging a pretty wide loop. I want it understood and plain to see who's boss here. Now, are you with me or against me?"

Lassiter timed a hesitation. "I didn't come this far to ride out with an empty poke. You call the shots."

The horses were stringing out. Fifty mounts and the pack animals. It made a long line. A serpent wriggling back into the unseen hills. The hooves dug a trough that a blind man could follow. There was no attempt to hide it.

There was no choice but to go along. Cassidy fell in at the end of the string. Lassiter stayed close, as close as possible to the man. If it was intended for someone to shoot him out of the saddle somewhere ahead he would make the target as hard as possible. Throughout the remaining hours of darkness a bullet could knock down Cassidy as easily as himself.

It was after daybreak that he should expect the attack. Still, he rode with the derringer in his hand, under the edge of his slicker.

Chapter FIFTEEN

Morning was mud and rain and more of both. The gap in the telegraph line had been found, new wire brought out, spliced. The keys were working again. Repair crews worked to heal the right of way with temporary tracks. Traffic was not yet moving, east or west.

That was someone else's job. Sidney Blood's job whirled around gold and outlaws. It had taken the whole miserable night to round up horses enough, to locate enough of his army, move it where the wrecked freight stood, forlorn, abandoned except for the cramped, unhappy, hogtied people in the dung fouled car.

Sidney Blood's temper strained on a weakening leash. The ground around the train was a morass churned by Cassidy's horses and the cattle herd that had been loosed. The steers were scattered to hell and gone. Some of them could be seen on the hillsides where a ravine cleft through. Of course the gold was gone. Finding the direction it had taken made more delay. Patrols thrown out in a wide circle to cut the outlaw's trail. Locating it brought further chagrin. Up the ravine. So bold and deep that they had assumed that the cattle had dug it in their escape.

When he turned up it Blood left behind a good deal done, and under difficulties. With the telegraph opened he had fired off a barrage of messages. To the army. The state governors. The sheriffs for miles around. All of the help he could call on was not enough to satisfy Sidney Blood for the upcoming manhunt. He was soaked, starved, tired. But mostly he was mad.

Contact with San Francisco had brought offer of a fifty-thousand dollar reward for return of the gold. For information leading to its return. Rewards doubled for Cassidy, Lassiter, any one of the Wild Bunch. Bait that Blood hoped would not have to be paid out. He wanted to find them and take them himself. Most especially Lassiter.

News of the increased rewards would have pleased Cassidy beyond his already pleased anticipation. Cassidy had gone along with Lassiter. Apparently. But from the first he had had his own idea of who would see the end of this trail. The party that would reach Mexico would be considerably smaller than the present fifty. The spoils divided would be less fragmented. Lassiter was not alone in his jeopardy.

He set a fast pace north, let his tracks reel out behind him. He knew Lassiter's suspicion, enjoyed it. Knew Lassiter rode with a gun hidden in his hand. Come daylight, Lassiter would wish he had eyes all around his head. That was fine with Cassidy. Let Lassiter expect. And keep expecting. The tighter Lassiter's nerves drew, the better repaid Cassidy would be for the humiliation at the Hole.

By noon the rain had stopped. The sun was out, hot. Fog evaporated from the canyons. The slippery mountain trail dried, then cracked. No move was made against Lassiter.

They rode steadily, with confidence. Sure of themselves here. This was their country, dominated by them for years. Outside justice never got near them in this territory. At sunset they rode into Colby. Openly. Bold. Lassiter was the only one surprised.

The town existed because of a crossroads, east-west, north-south. Its business was meager to serve a meager traffic. Corral, barn, blacksmith shop, a two story hotel and connected barroom made one block. Facing it were a general store, sheriff's office, jail, a fire house. The buildings one against the other, crowded as if space was at a premium in this wide plain.

On the cross street ran a gap-toothed row of shanty houses. In the ell on which these buildings turned their backs was a considerable depression, its steep sides used as a dump. Refuse, discard of all shapes, sizes, textures, degrees of disintegration sloughed down the slope. Ultramarine blue bottles still gummy with castor oil, whiskey bottles dyed purple by the sun, fragments of glass deepening toward dull orange, glittered through brittle leather, rusting cans, broken furniture.

Below the waste-fall, where the swale leveled, a handful of cribs huddled, shelter for the girls who worked the bar. All of the buildings were one color, pewter grey, weathered, warped, unpainted board.

The night's wetting had steamed off through the day. The road surface hard, dried mud crazing, curling in a drab mosaic, not yet broken into dust. Not that many horses had used it.

Cassidy's fifty wheeled in, milled around the livery door. There was not room in the corral for all the mounts. The first twenty filled it. The pack horses were driven into the runway, tied there. The overflow animals were dropped along the hitch rail, down the block.

Lassiter, at the end of the line with Cassidy, came up to find the men on the ground stretching, laughing, shoving, wrestling in horseplay. There was no sign of hurry, of urgency.

His mind went to Sidney Blood. Rain or no Blood would be well on his way. Probably by now would have picked up the trail. That deep, arrogant trail of Cassidy's. And a web of law would be springing up, surrounding them. Within twenty-four hours every road open to them would be blocked. The Outlaw Trail would be out beyond their reach.

What the hell was Cassidy doing? Where was he going? Soon there would be no escape route unless he went down in the ground, pulled the hole in after him. A hidden mine might do for that. A cave. But this was not mining country, cave country. It was flat as a griddle. Lassiter, waited, said nothing.

Cassidy was in fine humor. He detailed ten men to stay with the pack horses, led the rest in echoing tramp down the hollow sidewalk to the hotel. To the dining room. None of them had eaten in a day and a night. They were ravenous as wolves. Strangely there had been no protest from those left behind. They took Cassidy's arrangement as if they already expected it.

They ate in relays, sixteen at the tables, the rest taking advantage of the bar next door. Lassiter and Cassidy waited outside, listened to the din come over the batwing door, then joined the last group. The oilcloth on the long table was spotted, dirty. Flies swarmed hysterically over the food. No different from a thousand like places across the west. Every little isolated cluster that called itself a town had a duplicate. Except that there was food enough to fill the bellies of forty famished riders at least. The kitchen should not expect to feed forty in a month. Lassiter ate without appetite, automatically, of necessity. He did not know when he would eat again.

Afterward this group joined the others, again in the bar. There was no mention of a relief at the livery to let the men there come for food.

The saloon was bigger than the dining room, unadorned, functional. A long, plain counter ran from front to back on the side away from the arch. Poker tables filled the space between. Some looked to be permanent fixtures. More were makeshift, temporary. The chairs were mismatched, of many kinds, as if borrowed from different sources.

The girls were in shorter supply. There were only seven sprinkled through the crowd. None of them young, none good to look at. The painted smiles too heavy, bare shoulders oily, unwashed, the short dresses stiff with grime rather than starch. They made Hope seem queenly.

Two tables were occupied by strangers, not Cassidy's men. Four at one, five around its neighbor. A heavyset man with a sheriff's star on his shirt got up, made his way to the arch, shook hands heartily with Butch Cassidy, grinning. The other strangers watched, welcome in their faces.

So, Colby knew the Wild Bunch well. An outlaw town with an accommodating sheriff. And Cassidy must have sent word ahead that they were coming in. Lassiter wondered if this sheriff, these helpful people knew what trouble their friend was bringing in this time. It was beyond doubt that within a day, two at the most, Sidney Blood would thunder in here at the head of a Wells Fargo troop, asking questions, demanding answers, making things hotter than comfortable for those who sheltered the Wild Bunch.

Cassidy climbed to a chair, yelled to be heard, his arms sweeping the room.

"Set em up, boys. The night's on me. Give any man here

whatever he wants, all he wants. This is our night to howl."

It made no reasonable sense. Relax now? Celebrate? Get drunk? Even without considering Blood, one loose mouthed boast would tip this town off that half a million dollars in gold lay piled in the straw of their livery. A crowd full of whiskey was in no shape to protect that gold. No shape, if Blood showed up, to fight, even to escape.

Lassiter couldn't stop any of it. All day he had watched Cassidy, watched the line of riders, watched the side hills and the wide flat land. There had been no ambush, no try for him. He knew that it would come. Cassidy would never submit to his riding out with a single bar of that gold. It was too far out of the man's character.

Cassidy wanted to sweat him. That was plain enough. Lassiter's wariness was fine honed now. Cassidy moved away with the sheriff, joined the table, accepted a hand as cards were dealt. The game was desultory. The players' interest was somewhere else. On something they waited for.

Through the cloud of cigar smoke, the smell of heated bodies and whiskey Lassiter found another smell. The stink of death in the room.

The arch behind him was too crowded to move through. The bar was mobbed. The tables were filled, men standing behind the chairs, kibitzing. Lassiter went through to the back of the room. A table there had an empty chair, crowded against the wall. He wedged into it. The men there quit talking, looked at each other, shutting him out. They got up and moved away. He shoved the table forward, gave himself more room. From there he could keep track of the action.

A girl squirmed through the press, dodged the hands

that grabbed for her, came against the table. Her smile gashed her face.

"Want a drink with me, honey?"

He didn't look at her, watched the room. "Bring a bottle."

She went away, brought a bottle and two glasses, poured them full.

"You new in the Bunch? You ain't been here before."

"They come in often?"

"Pretty regular." She flopped to a chair. She did not touch her glass.

"Drink up."

She hesitated, covered, held the glass against her lips, waited for him. He raised his, cupped behind his hand. It smelled like a mickey. He tipped it against his lips, kept them tight. When she threw her head back, tossed her liquor down, he dumped his in his boot top.

He poured a second round, caught the sheriff's glance just leaving him, reached across the table to fondle the girl. She leaned toward him, fumbled, found her glass, found her mouth with it. Her eyes looked out of focus. While they were off him as she drank he made the second pretense of swallowing, palmed his glass, poured it after the first.

Her head went over, the temple hit the table. She didn't move again. Lassiter straightened back, looked astonished. The sheriff glanced that way again, Cassidy turned. While they stared at Lassiter a man at the bar crumpled to the floor. Another bent to look down and kept going. Lassiter did not appear to see them. He slopped more whiskey into his glass, spilled some, got the glass half way to his lips. His elbow on the table gave way, dumped him face down. He slid, rolled, landed on the filthy floor.

He lay doubled up, his eyes closed, breathed with laboring lungs. Throughout the noisy room quiet spread, pocked with querulous oaths, with jarring thumps against the floor. Chairs scraped. A heavy voice laughed.

"There you are Butch, just the way you ordered it. That's quite a sight."

"It'll make you rich." That was Cassidy. "The one under that back table is worth five thousand, Wells Fargo money. The rest will scale from one to three. A nice haul."

"Would be, if I didn't have to split it up all over town."

"Your business. Just you make sure none of them lives to talk, or you'll split a noose."

The heavy laughter. "I got that all set up. Let them come to, make a break. We'll be waiting up on the roofs. Like shooting carp in a barrel."

Boots crossed the room. Lassiter cracked his eyelids, saw Cassidy's boots, saw one swing back, had the second of warning. The toe slammed in his side. He lay inert, made no sound except the thick breathing. Cassidy's tone gloated.

"Bastard. You've got a sweet time coming to you."

Other boots came up. Lassiter's wrists and ankles were caught up. He was carried, swung like a hammock, out to the street, along it, in through a door, dropped on a wood floor. He lay quiet, on his face. Hands went over him, took his guns, stripped his pockets. More boots approached. The floor jarred with a second limp figure thrown down. A third. They kept coming, apparently ran out of room, began a second layer. Lassiter could not tell how many layers forty men made, but the weight crushed him flat, all but smothered him.

The sheriff was rattling papers, dodger sheets, Lassiter thought, and keeping a running count of profits aloud.

125

Lassiter admired the plan, the scope and simplicity of it. Cassidy was living up to his reputation. Ten men chosen to survive, help him get Blood's golden horde into Mexico . . . Lassiter made his bet that Mexico, South America, would still be the goal . . . get it aboard a ship. How many of the ten would live after that, he would not bet on. With forty of his old crew drugged, set up for mass slaughter, Cassidy's potential fortune leaped. With Lassiter among those sold to the sheriff of Colby, Cassidy was revenged on the man who had faced him down. It was a solid, efficient maneuver.

The cartage of live carcasses was finished. There was a period while they rested, laughed over the rewards Sidney Blood would pay them for this prime collection of wanted men. Cassidy was apparently gone. Lassiter smelled the smoke of fresh lit cigars. The sheriff said.

"Well, let's go watch the show." And the heavy boots of the men of Colby tramped out. A door closed. Left silence behind.

Lassiter moved, tried to move. The weight on him was heavy, shifting. Loosen it from one place and it sunk down in another. He was buried in bodies. It was like being buried in dry sand.

He got an arm crooked under him, tugged the other free of a wide belly that pinned it down, slid it beneath him. He shoved up, felt the weight against his shoulders give but not lessen. His spine arched backward. Dead weight filled the saddle, kept him down. His movement drew air around him from between the bodies, foul, sour, smothering.

He shifted his arms, got his elbows into his stomach, rocked forward, twisting. Head down, he forced his back up, dragged one leg in, got the knee doubled beneath him. He rocked again, brought up the other knee, rested, gathered all of his muscle, heaved his rump up. For a moment six hundred pounds hung on him, then sections of it slithered, rolled. His rump erupted through the corded bodies.

On his knees, he drew his torso, his head, out of the tunnel, looked about. There was no light in the immediate cell but a little came through the iron bars from the lamp in the office beyond. The wick was turned very low. He saw no one there, heard no sound.

The cell was small. The men were big, piled three and four deep in a sprawled tangle. On their feet they would have been jammed tighter than sardines in a can. Lassiter stood up, walked across the yielding bodies to the window at the rear. He tested the bars, found them too solid, looked out. The night was clear. It showed him nothing except the dump, the dark hollow.

He walked over the men again, went to the wall of bars. The door caught his attention. When he put his hand on it it gave, swung outward. That would be the sheriff's blind. A route left open to let the men try to escape when they waked. It would be considered within his rights to shoot down prisoners attempting a jail break.

Lassiter went to his hands and knees, crawled out of the cell, across to the office desk, stretched an arm up, turned the wick down. The light flamed for a second, went out. He crawled on, to the window fronting on the street. Close to the corner of the glass he raised his head enough to see through it.

There were men on the street. The sheriff, a dozen others. They ranged along the sidewalk, all looking one way. Up toward the livery. He could not see the building, but a path of light lay across the road, too wide to be anything except the open runway. Sudden laughter from the men came as something moving broke the light pattern.

Lassiter heard harness noises. Between the fence of figures on the sidewalk he saw the animals come down the street. Two Spanish mules, two more behind them as a team. The vehicle they pulled appeared. An army ambulance, trim, painted, red wheels unsoiled. Two uniformed figures rode the high seat.

It approached at a processional pace. Behind it rode an escort, spruce in regulation blue and campaign hats.

Butch Cassidy headed the escort. He wore the coat of a cavalry lieutenant. Cap set at a jaunty angle, shoulders squared, he made a fine figure of a soldier.

In front of the sheriff the train stopped. Cassidy got down, spoke to the man, waggled a warning finger in an army gauntlet, turned his back and rearranged his column. By twos, four men formed ahead of the ambulance, four remained behind. With the two on the seat all ten of Cassidy's elite were accounted for.

The outlaw swung up, raised a hand in salute, wheeled his horse to the head of the column, shouted his order. The little brigade swept out of Colby at a gallop, heading westward.

Lassiter did not know what the ambulance was supposed to be carrying. Whatever it was, he felt sure that Cassidy held written orders, forged, orders that would not be questioned if they were stopped in passing through Sidney Blood's lines.

The real load would be heavy, packed in a space beneath the floor. Yes, Cassidy had a flair, and scope.

Lassiter wondered if they had missed the two bars of gold now sunk in the mud under the cottonwood. They would not be linked to him, the pack horses had been too mixed up to tell who had handled which. But if the shortage had been noticed there would be a little less trust among this departing company.

Chapter SIXTEEN

The show was over. He could expect the sheriff, possibly others, to come back inside. He turned from the window, looked for guns. There were none. The rack had been stripped. The desk drawer held a clutter of reward dodgers, pencils, cigars, matches. But no guns.

Without arms he stood no chance in going outside. He had no chance except in lying dogo, waiting for a break. He went back in the cell, pulled the door closed, burrowed again into the wallow of drugged men, hid his head beneath a burly arm.

He heard the boots return, several men, coming to the cell, apparently looking in, turning away, settling themselves in the office for a night of pleasant forecasting.

Lassiter went to sleep.

After daylight a stirring of bodies waked him. Some came to their feet, walking on others, were sick, cursed their headaches. They made sour jokes. They had been thrown in jails for drunkenness before. It was a safe, cheap place to sleep off a celebration. This one must have been a beauty. It looked like the whole crew was here.

They began to shout for the jailor. They wanted out now. The rest had roused, were trying to get up. A general fight started, a battle of the lower layers for room to rise, against the friends standing on their faces, their bodies.

No one answered the shouts. They yelled for Cassidy. A panic began to grow. Lassiter crawled through legs, reached the bars. He could see the office, empty now. The thrashing around him pushed him tight against the grille, pinned him there. A shock wave surged toward the door. It gave under the pressure. Men lost their balance in surprise, fell outward, were stampeded over in the rush to quit the stinking cell.

They weren't suspicious of the unlocked door. It was the sheriff's courtesy to Cassidy. Let them leave whenever they were up to it.

They crowded out. Lassiter caught the bars, hung on to keep from being swept along with the pack. He shouted, kept shouting, warning them what waited outside. If they heard they paid no heed. He was not one of them. They had gotten used to ignoring him. They continued to.

The first rush crossed the office, yanked open the street door, stumbled through, stopped, blinded by the morning sun. They were pushed on into the road by the tide behind them.

Lassiter waited for the guns to cut down on them. The crash did not come. The only sound was the loud squabbling of men with bigger than usual hangovers. The cell cleared. The street filled. Lassiter was alone. He followed as far as the office, waited there.

A single shot exploded. A signal. All of the Bunch was now too far from the door to jump back to safety. The barrage roared, echoed around the office, rang in his ears like a knell. The tone of the yells changed, went high, fell silent.

Lassiter did not look outside. There wasn't time. He picked up the desk lamp, cracked the top from the bowl, flung the oil against the dry front wall. There were other lamps in brackets against the walls. One he splashed against the ceiling above the door, another against the floor.

He worked fast. If any of the sheriff's men came in now, Lassiter would be the forty-first man to die in Colby that morning. He opened the desk drawer, caught out reward dodgers in one hand, struck a match with the other, held it until the paper caught well. He raised it, passed it against the oil wet ceiling boards. As they caught he fired the wall, dropped the blazing paper to the floor.

The flames raced, ate at the rafters, the roof, blossomed up the wall, flowed across the floor. He threw more dodgers into them. Draft between the cell window and the door sucked the fire up. Smoke billowed with the flames.

There were new shouts now. Lassiter crouched near the door, within the smoke. It took time for Colby's men to drop off the roofs. One loomed abruptly in the doorway. He carried a rifle, an indistinct figure through the smoke.

Lassiter jumped on him, caught the rifle in both hands, twisted it, put a knee into the man's stomach, hard, doubled him backward. The man fell, stumbling over the sill, going down across the sidewalk. Lassiter ran over him.

The smoke shrouded the building front, rolled by a stiff wind. The building next to the jail flared, threw sparks through the air. The dark shapes of men tumbled off the flat roofs. A confusion of figures ran forward from down the street, hauling a red and brass fire engine.

Lassiter was a ghost, coming out of the smoke. No one recognized him. No one was thinking about prisoners just now. They were all supposed to be dead. A man running, on fire, was to be expected.

He ran across the street, carrying the rifle, reached the

livery, spun inside. His eyebrows, his hair were singed. His coat was smoldering.

He had glimpsed the quiet bodies sprawled all down the street, seen them without really seeing them. They would, he hoped, be incinerated beyond recognition. The sheriff could not collect the rewards for his massacre with corpses not identifiable.

Inside the barn there were horses, beginning to shy and rear at the smoke smell, doubling back on the Colby man there trying to drive them out of the runway. Lassiter moved through them, took the man by surprise, swung the rifle butt against his head as the other brought his gun up. The man fell down.

Lassiter tore off his coat. It was beginning to flame. He flapped it at the horses, saw them break, run for the door. He caught the line of the last one, flung the coat at a pile of loose hay, slung a saddle from a peg on a stall post, threw it on the horse. The man he had knocked down lay still. Lassiter lifted himself to the saddle, fought the horse under control. He would have liked to go out through the back door. There was none.

The hay pile was flaming, brewing heavy smoke that rolled through the front opening. A man's shout came through it to him. He wheeled the horse. It came around, up, on its rear hooves. Lassiter slapped its head with the rifle, gored his heels in its flanks. With a high cry it bolted, leaped through the flaming smoke. They ran down the man in the doorway, lunged into the street.

Behind him the roar of fire surged. The jail fire had spread. The block was burning. The livery fire would run through the buildings on its side. The town would go.

Lassiter's charge caught the men outside in full surprise. They were busy. Bucking their pumper into position against the town well. Organizing bucket lines. Their gun hands were not free. Some did not see him. Some stood gaping as the horse beat down on them. Two at the far end of the street saw, had time to set themselves, to draw.

One of them fired. The bullet cut the air beside Lassiter's ear. Lassiter's rifle exploded over the noise of the short gun. The man sat down as if he had been hit in the chest with an ax.

The second man fired. Twice. Lassiter had no time to return the shots. The horse was on the man, over him, knocking him into the dust in its terror, its hooves chewing into him.

They were past the fire, the action. The horse had its head, was running away. Lassiter did not check it. It raced at full gallop for three miles, finally slowed of its own accord.

Lassiter pulled it up, let it blow, stroked it to quiet, turned it to look back. There was no pursuit. All he could see of Colby was roiling smoke, bright flame rising as a huge ball into the sunlit air. He turned south. Through the mountains.

He was not out of danger. Colby might be too engaged to follow him, but the country ahead would be alive with Wells Fargo men. And he was in a hurry. He needed to reach the Hole in the Wall before Blood did.

Blood would fling his minions far and wide, but Sidney himself could be counted on to go to the Hole. His assumption would be natural. Always before, after a holdup, the Wild Bunch had dashed for the mountain fortress, dug in there, waited for the country to cool.

Lassiter rode by night, slept by day. He rode avoiding the campfires that dotted the hills where no fires should be. He avoided towns, mines, ranches. These were places Blood's men would visit, stake out. He had no food. He lived on water from the mountain streams, early berries from the little valleys. He had the rifle, but a shot at any game would sound his presence over too much distance.

Late the third night he came up the long valley to the canyon mouth. He smelled the smoke of a dead campfire, stopped until he was sure of its location, gave it a wide berth. It could be Blood. Or Blood could already be inside the Hole.

He rode the canyon with care. He was not challenged. Where it opened out at the top he waited in the deep shadow of the sentinel rocks, studied the community ahead. There was no light. No movement. He rode into the open, took the horse out of the street, across the quiet grass, well behind the store and cabins. Behind the building Johno Wade and Hope had shared he tied the horse, went forward on foot. He listened at the window, heard nothing, went to the door, eased it open.

"Who's there?" It was shrill with fright. Hope's voice.

"Lassiter. Be quiet. Anyone except the women in the valley?"

"No." The reed mattress rattled. "I'll make a light."

"Don't." He was sharp.

Sparks glowed red through the cracks in the stove. He went to it, lifted one lid, stirred the embers. They made a small glow that showed him the room. There was warm coffee on the back of the stove. He found a cup, filled it three times, rummaged through the larder box.

"You're hungry?" The girl came off the bunk, dug out biscuits he had not found. He wolfed them, softened them in his mouth with more coffee. She brought him cold meat, watched while he ate everything she put out.

Gradually the hollow cramping in his stomach lessened. He sat back in the chair, rolled a cigarette, smoked it, looking at the girl, through her, considering. The time was here when he must trust her, tell her what her part in the master plan was to be. It was the weak link. It was a chance. He had to take it. There was no other way to set Blood moving after Cassidy.

He stubbed the cigarette out in the empty tin plate, put his attention on the figure standing uncertain beside the stove. She appeared to be listening beyond the cabin. Instinctively she had not broken into his thoughts. Now she said.

"You came back alone? Did something go wrong?"

"It went fine."

She wore a long nightgown, high necked. In the dim warm light it made her look younger, unused, appealing. It brought a strong reaction in him, a need for her. This need of his loins, he had cursed it often as a weakness. Now he would bend it to his use. He must invest this frail will with a strength to carry forward for him. For him. Impress that indelibly on her.

He got up, went to her, took her face in her hands, kissed her long, deep. He found the fastenings of the gown, parted them, lifted it over her head. His want took over, pushed down the design of the mind. He carried her to the bunk, laid her on it, followed down the ripe body with strong hands. He joined her. The beat of passion drummed through them.

Spent, they lay in the dark, her arms around him holding him close. Her voice against his chest was muffled.

"You came back. You came back."

He played with her shoulder, fingered the soft pleasure of warm flesh, resisting bone beneath.

"I told you I would."

"I couldn't be sure. I was afraid Cassidy would . . ."

"Try to kill me? He did. He arranged a massacre for forty of the Bunch. After they got the gold for him."

She trembled. "He's crazy. Is he bringing it here?"

"No."

She stiffened, was shrill in indignant disappointment. "Has he got it all? Didn't you get any?"

"I didn't want it. That's not the money I promised you. Do you still want that?"

The sound pushed from her was not a word, was deep hunger.

"Enough to listen to me? Understand what I tell you exactly? Do exactly as I say?"

"Anything, Lassiter. But I'm not brave, remember that."

"Be just a little brave. Enough to act a little part. Talk to a man. He won't hurt you. He'll give you fifty thousand dollars."

She crowded against him like a child seeking safety. "Who?"

"Sidney Blood."

"Oh . . ." it was a moan.

"Fifty thousand dollars, Hope. Half of it for you."

She was silent. He waited it out. She whispered.

"Where is he?"

"He'll be in here tomorrow . . ."

Her movement cut him off. She was sitting bolt upright, clutching him.

"He'll trap you. You've got to get out."

He lifted up, kissed her, pulled her down to him again.

"He won't trap me. I won't be here. That's why you have to tell him where the gold is, collect the reward for the information."

"But I don't know where it is."

"Cassidy and ten men are hauling it in an army ambulance. They're going west from Colby toward Utah. To the Outlaw Trail. They're dressed as soldiers. If Blood hurries he can catch them at Yampa, at Ouray, or along Desperation Canyon. Repeat it after me so I know you've got it."

Mechanically she repeated, then shock came. "Turn Cassidy in? Me? He'd find out. He'd find me . . ."

Lassiter stroked her. "He won't find out. And when Blood finishes with him he won't be around."

"I'm so scared . . ."

He put his lips over her mouth, held her close. "Fear is good. It can help you do a good job. Make it work for you." When Blood comes, here's what you do. Tell him who you are, that you're Johno Wade's girl. He heard all about you in Spokane. He'll be more ready to believe what you say. He'll ask you where I am. Tell him I'm with Cassidy. Tell him you know where he can find the gold, but you expect the reward."

"He'd never give it to me."

"Oh yes he will. Just you believe it.

"Now. Don't talk in front of the other women. Don't let them know I've been here. Don't let Blood know. When you get the reward go to Denver, the Windsor Hotel. Use the name Austin. Write to me at Casper, then wait for me. Are you clear about everything?"

She went over it all, aloud. When she spoke of the reward her hand closed, as if it curled over the money. He didn't think he needed to warn her against trying a doublecross. She had not that much imagination.

He stayed with her for another hour. Then he dressed, left. He stopped at the store, took a knife, guns, a blanket roll of supplies. He found the hidden cash box, cleaned it out. Before daybreak he was out of the valley.

Chapter SEVENTEEN

He found the trail the sentinels used, rode up into the rocks, hid his horse. On foot he climbed where the horse could not go, to the nest of boulders at the crest. The ground there was packed by many boots, littered with the remains of many cigarettes. Here he squatted on his heels, watched the outer valley.

The sun rose, warmed the night chill from his shoulders, gradually drove back the shadow line from the land below. The wide green flat looked absolutely empty. Nothing moved that he could see. He cast back over what he knew of Sidney Blood's thinking and could find no reason to suspect that the agent would not come here. Sidney had always been predictable. Lassiter gnawed on a cold biscuit and kept to his vigil.

It was almost midday when he saw it. A little rise of dust in the distance where the trail should be. It rose and blew sideways in the breeze. Lengthened out like a growing snake. After awhile it stopped growing, came forward as a unit.

Several times he upgraded his estimate of their number.

When they were approaching the canyon mouth there looked to be near a hundred. Lassiter relaxed. That was Blood, alright, with an army, to break into the Hole. It had been done before by soldiers, although they had never taken the outlaws within. But it would be like Blood to advance in broad daylight, give Cassidy's crowd the chance to melt into the badlands, then make themselves at home and wait for thirst to drive the Bunch back out of the parched lava waste, pick them off as they came slipping toward the stream.

Blood spread his men in a long line across the canyon exit, out of gun range, as if to emphasize the strength of his force. He sent a single, lone rider forward. A sacrificial goat, Lassiter thought, to draw fire, to expose the position of a sentinel. His lips drew out in a near smile, watching the winner of this honor.

The man rode scared, his reins held high in one hand, his other on the horn. Nowhere near his guns. He came straight up the trail and under the brow of the crags. There was shadow there. He kept to the sun, in plain view. He rode slowly, stopped often, invited challenge. When no challenge came he rode on another space.

Stopping and starting, he entered the canyon proper. In the waiting silence Lassiter could hear the metal on his harness, the click of the horse's hoofs on the rock floor. When the lonely figure was out of sight he could be followed by his sounds. Each time he reappeared his shirt showed darker with increased sweat.

There was incredulity in the way he sat when he topped out and the high valley spread before him. He pulled up there, danced his animal aside into the rock shadow, made a long survey. Smoke curled blue from some cabins. Women moved across the sunny grass, going to the store, going from it. No male figure appeared.

Abruptly the rider kicked his horse around, raced back down the way he had come, rode to report to a mounted figure in the center of the line, who must be Blood.

Lassiter wanted a cigarette. He did not risk it. Even that little smoke might be seen in the clear high air. He looked down on Blood. Blood now raised his hand in signal, the line moved forward, shifted shape to a single file wide spaced. At a shout it broke into a gallop, charged the defile.

They would expect ambush of course. They would try to run through it. Blood had nerve to do it. His men had nerve.

They came headlong up the grade, expecting at every turn a crossfire of lead. They spilled headlong out onto the grassy swale. There they gathered, milling. Blood, Lassiter thought, would be congratulating himself that he had run his quarry out into a terrain where they could not long endure.

Lassiter moved his cramped muscles, shifted around to look down on the community. Women were scuttling into a clutch now, on the store porch. The Wells Fargo army rode toward them, Blood at their head. Hope came out of her cabin, ran to intercept him, stopped at his saddle, talked to him, jerking her head for emphasis, turned back, led him to the cabin. Blood got down and followed her inside. Lassiter risked a cigarette. No one below was paying attention to the heights.

Hope put the width of the room between them, faced around on Blood. Her eyes were enormous.

Blood's words hit at her, hard. "You're lying. They did come back here. Ran off to the badlands."

"No. Honest."

"Yes. And left you here to con me. Hid out behind your skirt. When did they go?"

She shook her head, stretched out a pleading hand. "They haven't been here. They never meant to come back. I know. I know." Hope didn't need to act. Her need to convince Blood had the clear ring of truth.

A weasel of doubt bit at him. "Where the hell else would they go?"

Her breath drew in sharply. "There's a reward, isn't there?"

"A big one. For the right information. After it's proven out."

"Would I get it if I told you where the gold is?"

He sneered at her. "Yes. After we recovered it. And twenty thousand more for Cassidy and Lassiter. What's your story? Where is it?"

"On the way to Utah."

"That's not enough to earn you a dollar."

"They're crossing the Yampa Plateau. To the Green River. Down the Outlaw Trail."

That struck a spark in Blood. He knew about the trail, the ghostly, invisible way along which isolated ranches, tiny settlements gave shelter, supplies, succor to men secretly traveling south, passed them from one to another hospitable stop. All the way to Mexico. He had never located it.

But he didn't believe her.

"They'd never get through. They wouldn't try. They're smart enough to know I've got a net of law all over that country."

She nodded, quick. "That's why they're dressed up like soldiers. They're taking the gold through in an army ambulance."

141

"How come you know all this?"

"Lassiter told me. Before he went off with Cassidy."

An answer made Blood smile. Lassiter had taken this woman away from Johno Wade. Now it sounded as if he were abandoning her here.

"He dumped you, did he? And you're mad and want to get even?" He turned away deliberately, reached for the door. "I'll think about it."

Her voice behind him came, desperate. "Take me with you. Out of here. The other women would tear me to pieces."

That was what he needed. Her fear. If this was just a show to lure him out of the Hole, no acting could match this genuine terror.

"We're taking all of you out. We're burning this rat's nest."

Through the afternoon Lassiter watched the buildings burn, watched the loading of the women into wagons. The long file trooped out. With Cassidy gone, forty outlaws dead in Colby, this would finish the Hole in the Wall.

At sunset the caravan reached the valley road. The wagons and a small detail detached, turned toward Bridge. Blood took the rest west, riding fast. At dusk Lassiter swung into the road behind them. He took care, but he doubted that Blood now would think of his back-trail. Blood's mind would not admit the idea that his nemesis was so nearby a shadow.

They pushed. Across the high Wyoming plains. Up over the Wind River mountains. Through the rough country downward toward the canyon of the Green. A sheriff's posse had saluted the ambulance and escort, passed it through. In chagrin they joined Blood. Twelve Wells Fargo agents in a group on a hill that overlooked ten miles of

trail had watched the detail camp at a stream, watched
their sunset drill, watched the eye of their fire through the
night, watched their soldierly order of departure in the
morning. A sheepherder had watched the blue band work
through his northbound herd two days before.

Blood drove his army. Cut short the unavoidable rests.
Half an hour behind, Lassiter used the embers of their
fires to boil his coffee, cook his food.

The meeting came without forewarning. Within the
canyon, against the river. The ambulance had broken a
wheel. Hurried repairs were being made, the wheel pulled,
a fire built to heat the rim and free it. Broken spokes dug
from the hub. Branches cut and shaped for replacement.
In the compressed heat there Cassidy was downstream,
watering the horses.

The noise of the river damped sound. Blood rode down
on them unseen. The trail was narrow, the uphill bank
steep, dense with timber. Someone fired too soon in surprise. Three outlaws were killed. The others ran, catching
up rifles, ducking into the trees. Cassidy spooked the
horses, sent them flailing up the hillside.

Blood flung an arm of riders up and around to outflank
those escaping, overrode the camp, took one band on down
to hold the trail where a cliff face made a barrier. The
rest of his army spread up to the crest, began a drive to
box the outlaws in, herd them down to Blood.

From the ridge Lassiter heard the spate of shooting. He
shook up his horse, rode parallel to the cut as far as the
jutting cliff, hid the animal, worked out to a vantage point
in the crown of rocks. He could just see Blood's blockade
beneath him, ten feet of the trail on that side. Downstream of the cliff he could follow it for a hundred yards.

Cassidy's last seven men had found him, found the
horses he had driven toward them. Above them they heard

the crashing of Blood's flanking party. Cut off from climbing, they had a single course left. Run Blood's blockade.

Lassiter was in time to hear them slant down through the timber. He saw them hit the trail almost on top of Blood, ride straight at him with blazing guns. Lassiter had to give him credit. Blood's band was firing. It could not stand against the rush. They came at him lying along their horse. Broke through. Two were knocked down there. Blood took after the others, disappeared behind the cliff nose.

When Lassiter saw them again there were three blue coated figures beating down the trail, three horses with empty saddles driving behind, Blood's group pounding after them. Within the area of his vision he saw these last pitch over, fall, lie still.

Three were unaccounted for. He could presume them to be dead in the blind spot. He waited where he was, watched Blood collect the bodies, the horses, repair back upstream. He felt dissatisfied, not knowing about Cassidy's fate.

Then he saw Cassidy. On foot. Climbing through the trees. The man was bedraggled, his clothes torn, but he was alive. He passed close enough that Lassiter could have shot him. He did not want him dead. He wanted him running, remembering always the glittering fortune he had almost had.

Later he watched a segment of Blood's troop, the Wells Fargo agent not among them, line out south. They would be on their way toward Mexico. Looking for Cassidy and Lassiter, who had not been found among the dead.

So much was done. He spent the night and the next day on the crags. Gave Blood time to collect his gold and clear his people from the area.

Chapter EIGHTEEN

Sidney Blood met Hope in Denver. Handed her the check in a ceremony with newsmen in attendance. He gave them an elaborate interview. Wells Fargo had wiped out the Wild Bunch, recovered what they had tried to steal. The fearful image was maintained. It should discourage others from trying. But he could not avoid admitting that Cassidy and Lassiter had escaped him, could only promise that both were being followed into Mexico.

He identified Hope at the bank, helped her deposit the reward. A painful process for him. Hope withheld a hundred dollars and went shopping. To look nice for Lassiter when he came. Bought a purple dress and hat with ostrich plume. Then she went to the hotel, wrote and mailed his letter. And waited.

It was only three days. The knock on the door brought her quickly to open it. She was smiling, face upturned.

Johno Wade stood outside. He carried a newspaper.

Shock froze her rigid. The smile turned grotesque. Wade put his hand on her face, pushed, followed her backward. He stopped at the bed, flung the newspaper wide on it, stabbed a finger at the big headline. He grinned down on her.

"Fifty thousand dollars, baby. What a haul we made."

She wanted to shriek. Her throat would not open.

His grin widened. "I got an idea we're gonna get us some more too. Who told you the boys was using soldier suits?"

She tried. The voice was ragged. "It was the plan. They talked about it at the store. I heard them."

Johno wagged his head ponderously. "No you never did, baby. Those suits been stashed there a long time. Nobody ever talked about them. Nobody knew when they were gonna be used. Only Butch. He used to say he'd tell us when we needed to know, and it would be after a job. Not before. So somebody got away from him at Colby and came to you. That would be Lassiter. And he wouldn't do it for love. Nosir. He had it all framed up for you to get the reward. Then he'd meet you someplace. Where?"

She couldn't speak. She shook her head. He slapped her. "You better tell me. You know what I can do to you."

"No. No. No I won't."

He laughed at her. "I guessed right, did I?" He knocked her across the bed, across the paper where he had read Blood's whole detailed story. "Well, you just wait right there. Johno's going to go make us some more money."

He wheeled out, locked the door behind him, tramped down the stairs. She crept up, went to rattle the door, could not pull it loose. She went to look out of the window. There was no roof below it. Only a stairway down the side of the building. Too far down to reach, too far to drop.

Johno Wade walked down Colfax to the express office. A wanted man, but he felt secure. He was polite to the clerk.

146

"Is Sidney Blood still in town, mister?"

"In the back here. Who shall I say . . .?"

Johno turned off the manners, knocked the man over backward when he came around the high counter, brushed by to the closed door.

Blood was at the table talking to Clyde Turk when Wade barged in. They looked up, startled. Before they could reach for guns Wade said.

"Lassiter. How much is he worth now?"

Sidney Blood put a rein on himself. Took his time reaching one of the new dodgers from the pile on the desk, holding it forward.

Wade read: *Lassiter. Dead or Alive, Ten Thousand Dollars.*

His tongue wet his lips. This was better than he expected. Blood read his face but his mood was still too sour, his latest failure too bitter to let him believe in Wade's anticipation.

"Don't tell me he's in Mexico. I know."

"No he ain't."

"Where do you think he is?"

"I don't know, right now."

Blood's frustration broke through. He heaved to his feet. "What the hell is this . . ."

Wade backed a step. "But I know where he'll be right soon."

"Damn you. Where?"

Johno Wade tucked his thumbs in his belt, swayed on his heels. "Right here in Denver."

Clyde Turk caught his breath. Blood snorted. Wade hurried.

"Yes he will. Hope's here. He'll come for her and the reward."

Blood looked full at him. "You're making a longshot guess."

"No. Listen. What she told you about the uniforms, she couldn't have known that unless he told her. After the holdup. It's a set-up between them."

Blood had no faith in it. But he didn't dare ignore it. "All right, let's go see her."

He followed Wade. At the girl's room he let him in. Hope lay on the bed in the exhaustion of fright, rolled away from sight of them as they cornered her. Blood pitched his tone to reasonable persuasion, sad accusation.

"Hope, I played fair with you, didn't I? I gave you the reward in good faith. Now Johno says you didn't tell me the whole truth."

She hugged her shoulders, did not turn back. Wade, blocky against the door as if he would cut off any possibility of escape, was nervous at Blood's obvious doubt. He stepped forward.

"I'll make her talk. I'll break her neck."

Blood turned on him, looked at him. Said nothing. He didn't have to. Johno subsided, stepped back. Blood went to stand above the bed, said with gentle emphasis,

"If you don't tell me the truth I will send you to prison as an accessory. Have you seen the prison in Wyoming? Do know what happens behind those walls?"

His answer was a shudder. The rumors she had heard must be worse than reality, but she could not be sure. She burrowed her head beneath the pillow. Blood yanked it away, dropped it to the floor. The vicious gesture pointed up the inexorable softness of his voice.

"I can do it, you know. I don't want to. You and Johno can both go free, wherever you choose. But I am going to have Lassiter. Whether or not you tell me, he is as good as dead."

He took her shoulder, pulled her over, held her face on his. She was no match for Johno Wade. Much less for the might of Wells Fargo, Sidney Blood.

Hardly knowing that she did it, she told him what he wanted to know, even to the letter she had written to bring Lassiter to this room.

Sidney Blood rejoiced.

Chapter NINETEEN

Lassiter did not go directly to Casper. He went back to the riverbank where they had stopped the train. The right of way had been repaired, the bridge rebuilt. Trains ran in and out of Bad Mountain as if their service had not been interrupted. Butch Cassidy's night of violence had left no mark.

In daylight Lassiter rode to the cottonwood, got down. With dry weather the mud had caked. It was hard. He should have brought a shovel. Instead, he used a pointed branch, scraped, dug. On his knees scooped out what he had loosened.

The bars were not at the depth he had left them. He went deeper. Hit rock. He began again, judging the direction in which shifting mud might have forced them. He was long at it.

They were there. He was not certain until he had broken both heavy lumps from the vice of soil, used his knife to gouge through the hard mud blankets, seen the dull gleam at the bottom of the scratches. Gold, of itself, possession of it, carries more impact than its simple monetary value. He put the bars aside. Sat back and rested.

With the reward Hope was collecting and these two gold bars, Wells Fargo was out of pocket near sixty thousand dollars. Enough to hurt. And Lassiter's share of it was enough to keep him going awhile.

He rode into Bad Mountain. It was not likely the company agents would be looking for him this close to Painter Canyon. The undertaker there built him a sturdy box big enough to hold one bar and a packing of gravel around it. When he had the box filled, the top nailed tight, he labeled it *Mineral samples,* addressed it to the Homestead mine superintendent in care of Arkland's sister on Vancouver Island in Canada. Despising the man, he would yet give him what he had promised. He was careful to pay his debts. It was a practice that had built for him a web of friendships that had often proved useful in keeping him out of Wells Fargo's eager hands.

He shipped the box by Wells Fargo. It was the only way to send it. And he liked the thought of the Express company carrying for him this missing bit of their own gold. The station agent accepted the box, grumbled at its weight, charged him twenty-one dollars. Lassiter paid him with money from Butch Cassidy's store at the Hole. Then he rode to Casper.

He spent an hour, walking the streets near the post office, watching doorways and windows. If Hope had betrayed him there could be a trap here. The area was busy, with no sign of tension. He walked into the single room and asked for mail. A bored postal clerk sorted through envelopes and handed one across the counter. He tipped the man, put the envelope in his pocket and left.

He rode carefully, crossed the river. He was not followed. When he was sure, he opened the letter, read it, smiling. Another step was finished.

He took time going to Denver. Traveled by night, came into the city by night. Soapy Smith controlled things here. The gamblers, the con men, the law. With money in his pocket a man could buy anything including safety. But even Soapy Smith could not buy off Wells Fargo. The agents went where they chose, made their own law.

If Hope had flawed her part, had roused the smallest suspicion, the town would be crawling with men looking for him. And she need not be aware of it. Further, knowing Sidney Blood, his mania for thoroughness, it could be expected that he would have the girl watched on principle. There could be trouble waiting.

Lassiter kept to the dark, the back streets. Rode softly, his hand on a gun. He did not approach the places he knew. Did not look for information. Took no chance on being exposed by a double-dealer already bought by Wells Fargo. It was not an unheard of happening.

He came to the hotel by the rear alley. It was checkerboarded bright and dark. Squares of light from windows made the spaces between darker. Along the ground it was black.

He got off the horse, tied it in deep shadow against a wall, drew both guns, walked into the alley. His feet felt each step before he let his weight onto them. He drew back from cans, crumpled papers, eased around rubbish barrels. He listened. Street noises filtered in, would cover the small sounds of anyone waiting ahead. He found the kitchen stoop jutting below the door, stopped to judge if there was any movement behind it, a man easing position, getting set. A prowling cat startled him, brushed hard against his leg, mewed, went on. It did not investigate behind the stoop.

Lassiter walked the length of the alley, stopped in shadow to look at the dim street. He went forward down it, along the hotel side, beneath the stairs of the fire escape. At the brighter cross street he looked around the corner.

No one seemed to be around the front entrance, no one behind the windows across the road. The glow from the front glass door suggested the lamps inside were turned low. He went back to the alley, opened the kitchen door, listened.

The room was dark. Warm smells came out to him. But no sign that meant life inside. He crossed the floor without sound, pushed back the door of the dining room. The light through the lobby arch showed him chairs, tables set up for breakfast. He shifted through them, put his back against the wall, twisted to look into the lobby. The night clerk was at the desk, reading a paper. The rest of the cluttered room was empty.

He went back to the kitchen, climbed the rear stairs, looked down the hall. No one was in sight. He filled his lungs, made up for the long stretch of shallow breathing.

Room twenty-six, Hope had written. He catfooted to it, stood almost against the door. No sound came out. No light seeped through the jamb. He holstered one gun, touched the knob.

He let it go, newly alert. The hall held many smells. One of them was burning tobacco. Stale tobacco odors steeped the walls. The other was fresh. He moved away from the door, tested the air. The smell was strongest where he had been, at the entrance of room twenty-six.

He drifted back, his footfalls light on the green carpet. At the end of the hall a window was open, curtains moving with a breeze. Outside it hung the platform of the fire stairway. He stepped out. The angle was not steep, the steps ran down the wall, passed beneath Hope's room.

153

But her window would be higher than his reach. If he could get footing on the wooden handrail he might make it.

He went down, took off his boots, stepped up to the slanting rail, clutching it with his toes, leaning across the treads, against the wall. He worked his hands upward. Stretching, he locked his fingers over the sloped sill, let go his toehold, hung against the wall. He was able, barely, to lift by his arms, bring his eyes above the window frame. He had a quick glimpse inside. Then his fingers slipped. He dropped back. In sock feet the sound of his landing was small.

He had not seen the girl. He had seen Sidney Blood.

Blood, sitting in a chair facing the hall door. A shotgun across his knees. No stakeout near the hotel, nothing that might warn Lassiter away. Only Blood, wanting to take him by himself. To blast him in half when he opened the door.

There could be one of two answers. Fifty thousand dollars was a lot for a girl like Hope to think of. Ten more on Lassiter's head would be riches beyond any dreams she could have had. She could have connived with Blood, made the try for the whole amount. Or she could have been discovered. Blood could have forced her to talk.

She was weak. Lassiter had chosen her because of that. Had thought she could not call up enough courage to cross him. But weakness could make her break easily too. He had to know which way it was. If she had been forced, he had a debt to pay. He would not abandon her if Blood was using her.

He went down the steps. They ended seven feet above the ground. He pulled on his boots, dropped away, stood to listen for a moment, went back to the alley, through the kitchen and dining room. At the lobby arch he leveled his gun on the clerk, made a near soundless whistle, beckoned with his head when the man looked up.

The man didn't want to come. He wanted to ring an alarm bell. Lassiter moved his head sideway. The clerk came forward.

Lassiter whispered. "The girl who was in twenty-six. Where is she?"

The clerk started, his eyes changed. "You're Lassiter?"

"You expecting him?"

The clerk flicked a glance at the stairs. "You've been up there? Mr. Blood didn't shoot. Did you kill him?"

"He's alive, waiting for me to push that door open. Where's Hope?"

"They went away."

"What they?"

"She and her husband."

"She hasn't got a husband."

Fright made the clerk's whisper rattle. "She has now. A big man, Mr. Wade, came in with Mr. Blood. They sent for a preacher and were married up there. I was the witness. Mr. Blood stood up with her."

Lassiter knew that his mouth was open. He closed it. "Where did they go? Think about it, what did they say?"

"I don't know. All I heard was the service, then Wade said they'd go out and get the money. They didn't come back."

Lassiter looked through the clerk. So Johno Wade had cut himself in on the fifty thousand.

"Yes. I see. Well, tell Sidney I was here, Say I'm sorry I couldn't wait."

He hit the clerk's head with the gun barrel. Not hard. Enough to knock him out for awhile only.

He left the hotel, went to his horse, looking at his chances of recovering the reward. In the morning he might talk to the banker, find out if Wade had transfered the funds to some other bank. He might get it from there. But Blood would know he was in town, would go to Soapy Smith and dangle the offer for Lassiter. Soapy would turn his forces loose. There would be no avoiding all of them.

He stepped to his saddle, rode out. Took the Fort Collins road. He would let them get away with it. Some you won, some you lost. His share would be Hope's wedding present. And even with Johno Wade she could count herself lucky. Marriage was beyond the reach for such girls as she. He would not have married her himself. There was no room in his life for one permanent woman. He looked up at the bright stars. Bright as gold. And wished her good luck.

It was finished, the long trail. The last part was a draw. Another draw with Sidney Blood. But he could take one more small satisfaction, and he was not wholly empty handed.

He camped before daylight in a sheltered draw, slept through the hot day. When he roused he took the last gold bar from his saddle bag, washed it in the stream, uncovered the mine mark of the Homestead mill stamped in one corner. With his thick bladed knife and a rock used as a hammer he cut into the soft metal, cut the corner out, patient, careful.

In Cheyenne he wrote his name across a piece of paper, wrapped the small fragment with the mill stamp in it, mailed it to Sidney Blood at his San Francisco office. He hoped Blood would open it, recognize it, with James Hume there to see. It was not much, but something.

He carried the rest of the bar in his saddlebag, headed west. On a high mountainside he had a friend working out a small mine. He would be glad to help for a few weeks. They would melt down the bar, break it up into sandy grains. The Homestead gold could be identified. It had properties different from the ore of other sources. But they could take their time, feed a little at a time into the new mined ore, ship it to the mint.

Almost five thousand dollars. A fraction of what Hope and Johno had got. But he was not as poor as Butch Cassidy, wherever he was moving. Butch could never go fast enough or far enough to shake himself free of his memory of half a million.

And he was not as hurt as Sidney Blood, with so much paid out and Lassiter still free.

EVERYTHING YOU ALWAYS WANTED TO KNOW ABOUT MARIJUANA

Latest Government reports estimate that 8,000,000 Americans regularly use pot at least twice a month. Many believe that this drug will soon be legal and will be as commonly used as beer or wine.

This book tells you what you want to know about pot. Explains the laws, the customs and methods of use, types of pot and how to recognize them, growing marijuana, using it in food and drinks, etc.

READ THIS BOOK AND YOU WON'T BE BURNED! NO MORE RIPOFFS!

BELMONT/TOWER BT • 50218   95¢

THE WOLFER
James Chaffin

Fiction: Western BT • 50209 75¢

Raw, savage Western. Running from an Army execution squad for a murder he didn't commit, Gary Hobart rode clear off the map, to become a wolfer in the outlaw-infested Montana badlands. Out there he learned to trust nothing but his guns and the razor-edged skinning knife that kept him alive. Soon he became as hard and merciless as the animals he hunted.

THE ANALOG BULLET
Martin Smith

Fiction: Mystery BT • 50210 95¢

An exciting, complex mystery novel by the author of GYPSY IN AMBER. U.S. Congressman Hank Newman found himself the victim of vicious attacks on his life by the committee that sponsored him, and an eerie plot to rob him of his identity. Authentic Washington backgrounds. Chilling suspense, explosive violence.

Belmont/Tower, c/o Tower Publications, Inc.
185 Madison Avenue, New York, New York 10016

Please send me the books listed below.

ORDER BY BOOK NUMBER ONLY.

Quantity	Book No.	Price
....	....	....
....	....	....
....	....	....
....	....	....
....	....	....
....	....	....
....	....	....
....	....	....

In the event we are out of stock of any of the books listed, please list alternate selections below.

....	....	....
....	....	....
....	....	....
....	....	....

I enclose $..........

NAME ....
(Please print)

ADDRESS ....

CITY .... STATE .... ZIP ....

(Send cash, check or money order)
NO STAMPS PLEASE

Add 15¢ for every Canadian dollar order. Please allow 4 weeks for filling orders. No C.O.D.'s please.